The Other

Even the book morphs!
Flip the pages
and check it out!

Look for other ANIMORPHS® titles by K.A. Applegate:

#1 *The Invasion*
#2 *The Visitor*
#3 *The Encounter*
#4 *The Message*
#5 *The Predator*
#6 *The Capture*
#7 *The Stranger*
#8 *The Alien*
#9 *The Secret*
#10 *The Android*
#11 *The Forgotten*
#12 *The Reaction*
#13 *The Change*
#14 *The Unknown*
#15 *The Escape*
#16 *The Warning*
#17 *The Underground*
#18 *The Decision*
#19 *The Departure*
#20 *The Discovery*
#21 *The Threat*
#22 *The Solution*
#23 *The Pretender*
#24 *The Suspicion*
#25 *The Extreme*
#26 *The Attack*
#27 *The Exposed*
#28 *The Experiment*
#29 *The Sickness*
#30 *The Reunion*
#31 *The Conspiracy*
#32 *The Separation*
#33 *The Illusion*
#34 *The Prophecy*
#35 *The Proposal*
#36 *The Mutation*
#37 *The Weakness*
#38 *The Arrival*
#39 *The Hidden*

<MEGAMORPHS>

#1 *The Andalite's Gift*
#2 *In the Time of Dinosaurs*
#3 *Elfangor's Secret*

The Hork-Bajir Chronicles
Visser

ALTERNAMORPHS

The First Journey
The Next Passage

ANIMORPHS®

The Other

K.A. Applegate

SCHOLASTIC INC.
New York Toronto London Auckland Sydney
Mexico City New Delhi Hong Kong

Cover illustration by David B. Mattingly
Art Direction/Design by Karen Hudson/Ursula Albano

ISBN 0-439-10679-6

12 11 10 9 8 7 6 5 4 3 2 1 0 1 2 3 4 5 6/0

Printed in the U.S.A.
First Scholastic printing, April 2000

The author wishes to thank Gina Gascone for her help in preparing this manuscript.

And for Michael and Jake

CHAPTER 1

Who am I?

Marco.

Not Tuan or Kevin or Rasheed.

You know, "Hi, I'm Marco."

If you yell out, "Hey, Marco!", chances are good I'll turn around. Respond. "What?"

You could also say that who I am is far more than a name. That who I am depends on your perspective. On where you're standing when you yell out to me.

Like, if you're standing out in the everyday world — in Red Lobster on all-you-can-eat shrimp night, on a downtown street corner, or in the mall — you'll see that I'm a slighty less than tall,

brown-haired kid. Come a little closer, like into my home, and you'll see that I'm also a son. A friend. And, on a very rare day, a decent dog-sitter.

If, however, you're standing in a very particular, very up-close-and-personal spot — like inside my head — you'll see that I am, in addition, a few other, less ordinary things.

Defender of Earth. Civilization's Last Chance for Survival.

Stuff like that.

Generally speaking, I make it a policy not to let people stand in that very up-close-and-personal spot. Superheroes tend to rack up a lot of dead friends and seriously damaged sidekicks.

That is one reason it's not a good idea for you to know much more about me than my first name.

The other reason anonymity is a good thing: the Yeerks.

The Yeerks. If it weren't for Elfangor, an Andalite war prince, I wouldn't even know about the Yeerks, aliens from a far distant planet. Wouldn't have been enlisted — me, four other kids, and another Andalite — to fight them. To try and stop their slow but constant infestation of Earth.

See, Yeerks are like slugs. On their own, they're blind, deaf, and mute. But in the brain of a host body, they've got eyes and ears and mouths. They're parasites, the Yeerks. Living off the minds and bodies of any creature they deem worth controlling. Gedds. Hork-Bajir. Humans.

And one — only one — Andalite.

Yeerks wriggle their way through the ear canal and into each nook and cranny of the brain. Open memories, raise hands, move legs. Once a Yeerk is in your head, you're totally and completely at its mercy. Saying what it wants you to say. Going where it wants you to go. Listening, silently, as it mocks your every desire and dream. Watching, impotently, as it enlists your mother or father or best friend into a life of slavery.

The right to privacy? Gone. The privilege of freedom? Gone.

What Elfangor did was give us access to Andalite morphing technology. This is our weapon, the ability to absorb through touch the DNA of a living creature and then become that creature.

We morph to fight and to infiltrate. To spy on the Yeerk cover organization, The Sharing. And occasionally kick Yeerk butt.

We become whatever we need to become. Elephant or gorilla or grizzly. Tiger or wolf or cockroach. Cheetah or polar bear or even Hork-Bajir.

All of which makes that "who are you" question a whole lot more complicated for me than for say, about 99.9 percent of folks on this planet.

That remaining .1 percent — those would be my friends. The other Animorphs. Jake. Cassie. Rachel. Tobias, the guy who lives as a hawk. Ax, Elfangor's younger brother.

Obviously, there are a lot of issues we have to deal with. Issues far too complex for the six of us to waste a lot of time thinking about. Or maybe we've become far too complex for them to matter too much anymore.

In almost every way you can imagine, we've pretty much been there. Done that and bought the T-shirt and poster. If anyone from Guardian or Prudential knew the truth about us, we'd never, ever get health insurance. Forget about life.

Me and my friends, we are the definition of extreme living.

We are the definition of high risk. We don't need to sign up for a class at the local community college or pay some slick shrink 150 bucks an hour to tell us we're not realizing our potential.

Our potentials have been realized up the wazoo.

See, this war comes down to life or death. Freedom or slavery. Dignity or abject humiliation.

Failure is not an option.

Bottom line — we're here to serve. It's not only about us. It's about you, too.

That's why, every once in a while, it's real nice to be alone. Shut out the world and do something just for me. Something totally and completely self-indulgent and soul-numbing. Something that requires almost no effort, physical or intellectual.

The house was empty. Dad and Nora were at a PTA meeting. Euclid was spending the night at the vet, recovering from some minor doggie surgery. Jake and Rachel were off at a family thing. Cassie and her mom had gone to some big veterinary conference at The Gardens. And I guess Ax and Tobias were doing whatever red-tailed hawks and aliens do on an off night. I just knew I was blissfully alone.

I lay back on the living room couch. Stretched like a lazy old cat. Reached for the remote on the coffee table.

Nothing good on the tube. Perfect. I channel-surfed, past *SpongeBob SquarePants* and a minor league baseball game. Past *Two Fat Ladies* on the food channel. Past a documentary on beetles.

Ah! *Unsolved Mysteries.* Cool. The Loch Ness Monster. Bigfoot. Aliens from outer space . . .

Mr. Fake-Spooky Host looked wide-eyed into the camera. "When we come back after these messages, we'll continue our in-depth investigation

of legendary creatures with an amateur video made just weeks ago, right here in . . ."

I hit the mute button and waited. Hummed some Kid Rock. Yawned. Bit a hangnail. Seven commercials later, the show was back.

And then the world fell apart.

CHAPTER 2

It was just a blue blur moving across the screen. Not much more than that. A small piece of videotape taken with an unsteady hand in terrible light conditions.

But it was enough.

My foolproof danger alarm went off. Loud.

"Could this be proof positive of the existence of the magical unicorn of medieval lore?" the host intoned. "Or could this strange blue creature be the mighty centaur of Greek mythology? Let's take another look."

I hit the power button and the screen went gray.

One look had been more than enough.

The image was blurred but unmistakable.

Andalite!

I scaled the stairs to my bedroom two at a time.

This was bad. Really bad. A serious breach in security. The beginning of our end . . .

A good bazillion citizens of the United States of America, and who knew how many people in how many other countries, had just gotten their first glimpse of a bona fide alien.

Eighty, maybe ninety percent of those viewers would be excited for about thirty seconds — at least until the next silly monster after the next silly commercial.

Ten, maybe twenty percent of those viewers would recognize the blue blur for what it was. Not a unicorn or a centaur.

An Andalite. Here. On Earth.

And it could only be Ax.

Okay, Visser Three and every other Yeerk with a host knew of the "Andalite bandits." The ones who formed the small but unrelenting resistance to the Yeerk movement.

But others — humans not controlled by Yeerks — didn't know. And they couldn't. Shouldn't. It was too dangerous, too risky. Bad for Ax to be taken prisoner by the visser. Worse for him to be taken for study by the government.

Not everybody in "the agency" was as fair-minded as Scully or Mulder. Some were even Yeerks.

Ax would not be taken. I would make sure of that.

A thousand fears and anxieties ran through my head, almost as quickly as I ran up the steps and into my room.

I had to get control. Focus. Maintain that focus.

I went to the bed. Arranged the pillows under the blankets to look like a sleeping kid. So my dad and my stepmother wouldn't know I was gone. Again.

I stripped down to my morphing suit. Tossed jeans, T-shirt, and sneakers into the pit that is my closet. Tore open the window. And began to morph.

The goal: rapid transportation.

PING! PING!

I winced. The beginning of talons, where my toes had been only a few seconds ago. I watched as the rest of my feet and ankles withered, shrunk, and suddenly became the bird's incredibly strong, gripping feet. Three long fleshless talons facing front, one facing back.

No way those feet could support my thick human legs. I was going down.

THUMP!

I was definitely down. But I'd fallen on my back. I lifted my head and watched as my legs blackened and shriveled up into my body like two sticks of beef jerky being sucked up by a gnarly old cowboy.

Right then I vowed never ever to eat a Slim Jim again.

In spite of what you might think, morphing doesn't hurt. It's just disgusting.

But still, I watched. As if I could hurry the process by witnessing it. Fingers — curling into my palm. Tanned human flesh lightening to gray and then disappearing under a flat, three-dimensional tattoo of feathers. Then arms sprouting feathers in a fury. At the same time, arm bones shrinking, hollowing, reshaping. Becoming wings.

My mouth and nose melded together, hardened to form a curved and deadly beak.

Internal organs? I felt approximately twenty-five feet of human intestines smoosh and squish down to a bird's tiny digestive tract. My slow and steady human heart surge into the manic, pulsing heart of the bird of prey.

No longer human. No longer tall enough to see the unopened notebooks scattered over the desk. The handful of empty bubble gum wrappers I should probably throw away. Close enough to the carpet to see boulders of cookie crumbs and single strands of curly poodle hair. Ugh.

I was an osprey. The animal that had become one of my earliest morphs. Not a bird with the greatest night vision but vision a heck of a lot better than a human's. Vision good enough to get me where I was going.

Ax's scoop.

I hopped up onto the windowsill. Glanced sharply around with beady eyes to be certain the house wasn't being watched. And flapped into the night air.

CHAPTER 3

Ax was at "home."

And he had company perched on a nearby branch.

<Tobias!>

<What brings a guy like you to a place like this?>

<Nothing good.> I flared my wings and landed on the soft grass and dirt. Started demorphing.

<When is it ever good when one of us just shows up, all unexpected?> he added.

I didn't answer. Tobias has been big on rhetorical questions lately.

Besides, at the moment, I didn't have any of what Ax would call "mouthparts."

But I did have eyes. Ax's TV was on. But not on the station I'd been watching.

As soon as my lips were formed I looked directly at Tobias. Then at Ax. "Our buddy Ax here is a star," I said brightly, brushing dried-out pine needles off my bike shorts, wincing when a sharp stone bit into my tender human foot.

I told them what I'd seen. When I'd finished, there was silence.

It was Tobias who spoke first. <Well, Ax?> His thought-speak was hoarse. Almost anxious. <Is it possible?>

Ax hesitated. Turned his main stalk eyes to look behind him, toward the deeper woods.

<Anything is possible,> he said.

That was not what I wanted to hear.

<I guess we need to get a copy of that episode,> Tobias said.

"D'ya think? Really?" I said, rolling my eyes. "Okay. Listen. We don't have time to wait around for the rerun or to send a check to the station in order to buy a copy. We just can't risk waiting."

<That's true,> Ax said as he stepped to his television setup. <But we don't have to wait.>

"Did I miss something? 'Cause I'm definitely not understanding you."

<Ax tapes everything,> Tobias explained. <On every channel. He's set up a CD-ROM thing to

the VCR — or something like that. Anyway, it works.>

<Marco, I believe this is what you are looking for.>

Ax stepped back from his small pile of equipment. With a remote, he fast-forwarded through the thirty-minute show until he reached the segment.

All twenty seconds of it.

Ax froze the final frame.

More silence. This time, I broke it.

"Is it you, Ax?"

Ax briefly focused all four eyes on the screen before sweeping those on stalks around the perimeter of the scoop. Wary now.

<I cannot tell from that angle.>

<Play it back in slow motion,> Tobias suggested. <Frame by frame.>

Ax did. To me it still didn't make any difference.

It could have been Ax.

It could have been any Andalite.

But the only other Andalite we knew of on Earth was Visser Three. No way would he ever be careless enough to allow himself to be caught on film. Besides, he was never without a phalanx of bodyguards.

Unless . . . unless he *wanted* to be seen by thousands of couch potatoes. But why?

"Ax-man. Is there any way to fine-tune the image?" I asked.

<No. I cannot clear the resolution on a non-original piece of film or video.>

Tobias swooped off his perch and landed, gracefully, a few feet from the television screen.

<You don't have to,> he said. <It's not Ax.>

"So it's the visser," I said. "Well, that's a little beyond weird."

<No. Not the visser.> Tobias turned his incredibly intense hawk eyes on us. <Kids, I think we've just discovered another Andalite.>

Ax pulled his shoulders back. <Is it . . .>

<It's not Estrid. Sorry, Ax. Not Arbat, either.>

"Alrighty then. Who?"

<This guy's new. And he's got one real obvious distinguishing feature. He's got only half a tail.>

<A *vecol*!> There was disbelief in Ax's voice. Something else, too. More than his normal, well, arrogant tone. It sounded like disgust.

"Excuse me?" I asked.

<He is disabled. A cripple,> Ax answered coldly. <And his presence here will obviously be a problem.>

"Yeah," I agreed, looking back to the hazy image on the screen. "The Yeerks get ahold of him, they've got another morphing Andalite on the team. Not good."

<No. The Yeerks would have no use for his *body.* He is completely useless as a host.> Ax waved his frail hand in a dismissing motion. <Without a tail blade he cannot fight. And it is obvious this *vecol* is incapable of morphing or he would have restored his tail from his own healthy DNA.>

"So, Ax, how do you really, *really* feel about this guy? Let me take a wild guess." It sounded nasty. I meant it to.

<Marco,> Tobias said. <Seems to me this, uh, guy, could be useful to the Yeerks in another way. He's got to have information the visser wants.>

"Which means wherever he is, we get to him first. Unless we're too late. Which I'm not even going to think about."

<Right,> Tobias agreed. <Best-case scenario, he becomes an ally.>

Ax made a sound that was way close to a snort. <A *vecol* as an ally? Marco, was that meant to be humorous? Because it was not.>

I grinned. Folded my arms across my chest. "No, Ax. It wasn't meant to be 'humorous.' What's with you? What's your problem with this guy?"

Tobias interrupted, <Let's get going. We're going to need to talk to Jake and the others. We can deal with this stuff later.>

I took a deep breath. Gave my hair a good

yank, straight up. Spoke. “Yeah. It’s time to find us an Andalite. Oh,” I said, looking blandly at Ax. “Let’s not forget one other possibility here. In spite of the famous-throughout-the-galaxy Andalite honor, this guy could, as we know, quite possibly be a traitor. The whole videotape thing might be a trap for us unsuspecting, bighearted humans, who respond to creatures less fortunate than us with empathy and kindness.”

<That is true,> Ax said, while staring back at me with his main eyes. <It might very well be a trap.>

CHAPTER 4

Tobias led us to the clearing that he was pretty sure was the same place the Andalite had been caught on tape.

Something about the slope of the field and a pine tree partially destroyed by lightning had given him a clue. If Ax is our personal clock, Tobias is our personal cartographer and wilderness guide.

Maybe we should have tried to contact the others first. Waited until morning. But we didn't. Didn't even discuss the possibility of delay. It was starting to get dark. So, I went owl for some serious night vision capability and we were off on what was intended to be a simple reconnaissance mission.

We circled above the clearing, Tobias, the most experienced flyer, swooping as close to the ground as he dared. Alert to every movement. Every twitching blade of grass and swiftly disappearing tail of mouse or vole or whatever skanky creatures run around after bedtime.

<What, exactly, are we looking for?> I said. The world was lit up before me, amazingly clear. But I didn't see anything that shouted "danger!"

<Anything out of the ordinary,> Tobias said. <Signs of a struggle. Trampled earth. Dried blood maybe.>

But there was nothing. If anyone, man or beast, had made tracks there in the last few days, they'd since been swallowed by the ground, which was still damp from the previous night's heavy rain.

No evidence of foul play.

After almost twenty minutes of futile searching, I suggested we head home. Get some sleep. Get in touch with Jake and the others.

<We should demorph,> Ax suggested. <We have been in morph for almost ninety minutes.>

I'm not big into taking unnecessary risks. The idea of morphing in such a dark and lonely place. Especially without having the others around to watch our backs. Nope. The thought did not thrill me.

I was even less thrilled by the idea of getting

stuck with a flea-and-tick problem for the rest of my days.

So while Tobias kept aerial guard, I landed on the ground, close to the west rim of twisted pines, and quickly began to demorph. Ax, on the other hand, was still descending, several yards away. We thought it safer to stagger our morphing.

SCHLOOP! SCHLOOP!

Okay. No wings. But no arms yet, either. Great.

SPLOOT! SPLOOT!

Shriveled arms. Little stubs of fingers at the tip. Slowly, slowly filling out.

With my still-owl eyes I saw Ax beginning to demorph.

Decided I'd rather not watch.

Flipped my eyes to the right. Saw a furry old possum. And . . .

<Marco! Ax!> Tobias called frantically. <Get out of there, now!>

Too late. I was three-quarters human.

It had finally happened. We'd been too careless. Underestimated the enemy.

We were really dead.

And for some reason, I looked over at the possum.

It doubled in size.

Doubled again. Again!

Its gray fur began to turn blue, almost like the color was being poured down each strand from a zillion small vials. Or like one of those goofy pens that change color when you tilt it back and forth.

It didn't take a rocket scientist to realize this was no ordinary possum.

It was an Andalite.

It was not Visser Three.

And it was not the one we'd seen on television, either.

This Andalite had a monstrous tail, long and thick. And at its end, a blade that, to my terrified eyes, looked a lot like that scythe thing the Grim Reaper carries.

I was barely finished demorphing when the Andalite started to walk toward Ax. His tail sliced the night air menacingly, blade glinting in the light of the almost full moon. Each hubcap-sized hoof clomping the dewy ground, sending little clods of soil flying. Field mice scurrying.

This was no — *vecol.* This guy was massive. Bigger than any Andalite I'd ever seen. Bigger than Ax's brother, War Prince Elfangor-Sirinial-Shamtul. Bigger than Aloth-Attamil-Gahar. Bigger even than Alloran-Semitur-Corrass, host body to Visser Three.

Shoulders like a fullback. A chest that was cut like a competition-level bodybuilder. Arms that, except for the blue fur, could pass for those

of a middle-weight champion. Even the usually small and delicate many-fingered Andalite hands were broad and toughened. Like those of a carpenter or construction worker.

Most disconcerting: From the almost human waist to the rounded, deer or horselike haunches, the guy looked like a Clydesdale. A *really* big one.

No way was Ax, a kid, an *aristh,* a match for this guy. Ax is good, a seasoned fighter, but you would have to have been downright dopey not to see that this guy could kick Ax's butt with one casual twitch.

I'm not a betting kind of guy, but if I were, I'd have laid my money on Mr. Macho for a first-round slice up.

But the Andalite didn't strike Ax. Or me.

He stood there, not five yards away. He was ignoring me but he *was* staring at Ax, who was now also back in his natural form, tail blade cocked. The big Andalite seemed to be waiting for something. For Ax to strike first?

<Okay, guys, this is bad,> Tobias said privately, so the Andalite couldn't hear. <But I don't think he's seen me. I'm gonna try to catch him off guard. Before he makes a move.>

Nervous and unable to answer Tobias, I shot a glance at Ax.

He stood perfectly still, mimicking the ready stance of his opponent. Waiting for a first move.

<Tobias,> he said, his thought-speak calm and low. <I do not think . . .>

Too late!

"TSSEEER!"

Tobias swooped down from the night sky! In the white light of the moon, talons suddenly extended for attack, he looked like a hellish feathered demon.

"TSEEER!"

The Andalite flinched. Flinched! Took a slight, faltering step backward. Twitched his stalk eyes upward and kept his main eyes on Ax.

Yes! Tobias was going to do it, hurt or distract him enough to allow us the advantage . . .

FWAPP!

With blinding speed and accuracy the Andalite's massive tail cut Tobias out of the sky.

And then there was a sickening thud as Tobias hit the ground.

"TOBIAS!"

CHAPTER 5

I started running toward Tobias's lifeless body. But a warning glance from Ax held me in my place. What was I going to do? Maybe, at least, retrieve Tobias before his body could be sledgehammered by those monstrous hooves.

I could morph, I thought wildly. *I could . . .*

<Do not do anything, Marco. Do not say anything.>

Now Ax was a mind reader? Forget it. I'd go gorilla . . .

CLOPCLOP CLOPCLOP!

The Andalite galloped at Ax.

CLOPCLOP CLOPCLOP!

Ax galloped at the Andalite.

Ax lunged.

FWAAAP!

Swiped at his opponent's throat.

And missed.

Now the big Andalite had full advantage. Before Ax could set up another shot . . .

THWAAAP!

He was struck with the flat of the Big Blue's blade. And then Ax was on the ground.

The Andalite stepped back to allow Ax to climb awkwardly to his feet. Then he calmly pressed his broad tail blade to Ax's throat.

<Visser Three,> the warrior said, his thought-speak thick with contempt. <At last we meet. I was unaware of the fact that you were such a puny, worthless adversary.> He tossed one eye stalk in the direction of Tobias, still motionless on the dew-soaked ground. <It is no wonder you send your minions to do the work of a true warrior!>

<*I* am not Visser Three,> Ax replied, with an admirable amount of dignity, considering the huge tail blade pressed to his throat. <I am Aximili-Esgarrouth-Isthill.>

Half a second passed. The Andalite appeared to be processing that bit of information. Grappling with it.

<Younger brother of Prince Elfangor-Sirinial-Shamtul?> he said finally. Doubtingly.

<The same.>

Now the Andalite's thought-speak became stronger. Challenging. <You were on the great Dome ship. In its last, fateful battle. You survived the crash?>

What was this? I felt like a wallflower at some bizarre Andalite Academy reunion. And while they chatted, Tobias . . .

<Yes,> Ax said. <Although I begged to be allowed to fight, I was sent to wait out the battle in the dome. Until quite recently, I was under the impression I was the only one who had survived. Perhaps I have been mistaken. I witnessed the video of the *vecol* . . .>

<The *vecol*!>

The roar of the Andalite's angry thought-speak was deafening. It actually made my head hurt. I watched helplessly as he pushed his tail blade even deeper into the skin of Ax's neck. Drawing a small trickle of blood.

<His name is Mertil-Iscar-Elmand,> the Andalite went on, in a slightly more normal tone. <And you will do well to remember that, *aristh*.>

Ax is no fool. When he spoke, he kept the tone of his thought-speak neutral. <I have heard of this Mertil-Iscar-Elmand. The fighter pilot. I have heard of the many honors he received while participating in various battles. And whom do I have the honor of meeting now?>

This was insane. Ax definitely had a career as

an actor alongside Gwyneth Paltrow in *Shakespeare in Love.* Or maybe as a diplomat. I was so freaked out that I was about to wet my pants, and Ax was acting like a hero in a witty drawing-room comedy or something. Talk about grace under fire.

<I am Gafinilan-Estrif-Valad.>

Ax's four eyes showed a sudden respect. His thought-speak revealed a note of excitement.

<I have heard of you, also. Your reputation as a fighter pilot is one of the finest in the history of the academy. Your career sets an example every *aristh* would be well to follow.>

Gafinilan removed his tail blade from Ax's neck. He looked embarrassed. Awkward. Not displeased by Ax's praise but not pleased, either. He averted his main eyes from Ax's own.

<Commander Gafinilan,> Ax continued, excitedly, <recently, I was made aware of the fact that the Andalite fleet has been diverted from its mission to quell the Yeerk invasion on this planet. Instead, the fleet has been sent to deal with the Rakkam Garroo conflict in the Nine Sifter. There will be no special forces deployed to help my comrades stop the Yeerk conquest of planet Earth. You must help us . . .>

<I *must* do nothing,> Gafinilan retorted bitterly. <I am no longer a warrior, Aximili-Esgarrouth-Isthill. My sole purpose now — indeed, my duty

and my responsibility — is to care for Mertil. As you have noted,> he added, his tone darkening, <he was badly injured in our last battle. The one that stranded us on this planet, so far from our home.>

Ax seemed about to protest.

<Leave us in peace,> Gafinilan commanded. Quietly. No room for argument. <If you do not, if you try to prevent me from fulfilling my task, I swear by the memory of my parents that you will die.>

I stood as still as I'd ever stood. Almost at attention. Stiller even than I'd stood at my own mother's funeral. Only this time, I was afraid that if I moved so much as a hair I'd be killed.

Rebellious, nonmilitary-issue behavior from an Andalite should not have struck me — us — as unusual. Or disturbing. Not after the stories we'd heard about Alloran on the Hork-Bajir planet. Not after knowing that Elfangor had broken one of his society's strictest laws. And especially not after our recent encounter with Arbat-Elevat-Estoni, a soldier and thinker driven mad by war.

Still — there was something awful and dark and desperate emanating from this stranded alien soldier. I had no doubt whatsoever he meant what he'd said. That he'd kill us if we came looking for him and Mertil.

Unless . . .

Out of the corner of my eye I saw Tobias stir. Was outrageously grateful he was alive. Willed him to be still, not to call attention to himself.

<Now, go, *Aristh* Aximili. Take your — friend — and leave this place. Visser Three will be here at any moment. And he will not be as merciful as I have been, I assure you.>

<Sir . . .>

<For your own good, Aximili!> Gafinilan said harshly. <Forget that you ever saw me. Forget about Mertil. That is an order. Forget.>

Gafinilan turned away from us, all four eyes forward as he walked back toward the dark woods. Away from the revealing light of the moon.

At the edge of the woods, he stopped. He did not turn around, not even his eyes.

<I wish you luck on your mission, Aximili. You and your comrades. Even though it is hopeless.>

CHAPTER 6

We followed Gafinilan. Of course. He probably knew we would.

And now I knew he wasn't going to do anything to us.

Gafinilan had us trapped and had knocked Tobias out, but he had let us live. We wanted — needed — to know why.

And there was something else.

The Andalite had seen me demorph. At least, I was pretty sure he had.

Maybe he hadn't seen the *entire* process. How great were a possum's eyes, anyway? I had no idea. Maybe he thought he'd missed something, that I'd already morphed from my natural Andalite body to human . . .

Who was I kidding? He had to have seen it all. My gut told me that. Besides, why would any guy with a tail blade morph to a weak-limbed, soft-skinned thing in the face of trouble?

It didn't matter much what he found out about me from this point on. As long as he didn't live long enough to tell it.

I went wolf, fast. Ax went harrier. While we morphed, Tobias checked himself out and decided he was okay. So, even though he was still a little wobbly, he took off after Gafinilan.

<He's moving fast, guys. I can't get up too high or I'll lose him. Tree cover is too thick. And I'm having trouble manuevering in this low light.>

I took off. With the wolf's superior sense of smell, with its amazing stamina and agility, we stood a decent chance of tracking Gafinilan. I hoped.

<Just stay with him, Tobias,> I called. <We're on our way.>

I tore through the dark mass of trees. It was like racing through a maze to reach the prize in the center — a prize you really didn't want 'cause you knew it was dangerous and maybe even lethal. A prize you'd have to destroy before it destroyed you. But a prize you had to have, no matter what.

Around and past dark green pines and small masses of rock. Under heavy, low-hanging

branches. The air chilly and damp, masking certain odors and altering others. Still, I was pretty sure the wolf's keen nose detected the big Andalite. I ran.

Above me, Ax and Tobias did their best in the lousy flying conditions.

But their best wasn't good enough.

<He's gone!> Tobias cried suddenly. <I can't . . . he was just up ahead . . . then nothing!>

I stopped under the branch where Tobias perched. Thrust my nose at the ground, desperate to locate Gafinilan. Raised my head and sniffed the air. Ax came swooping down close by.

<It's like he just disappeared,> Tobias said.

<I'm getting next to nothing,> I added. <At least, no clear direction.>

<As much as I do not want to mention the possibility,> Ax said, <perhaps there is an entrance to the Yeerk pool complex hidden somewhere near. Perhaps Gafinilan passed through . . .>

<Wait!> I said. I padded silently about a yard into the deeper wood, using all the wolf's senses. <He went this way. It's faint but . . . look!>

It was some kind of cave or passage. About another three yards to the right. Not easy to spot unless you were looking for it. The entrance was low and narrow and almost completely hidden behind the sweeping branches of an evergreen.

<Ten to one that's where our Andalite friend disappeared to,> I said. <Looks like you were right, Ax-man.>

<And it looks like we're not alone,> Tobias said.

Something was coming out of the cave.

Someone. A human. A man.

He stopped just outside the cave's entrance. Looked around carefully. Suspiciously. As if he were expecting to find spies hidden behind the trunks of trees.

He was average.

Nothing remarkable about him at all except his total and complete averageness. Good-looking. Average height and weight. Middle-aged, maybe thirty-five, maybe forty-five. Hair halfway between blond and brown, halfway between short and long. He wore a pair of nondescript jeans, a dark plaid shirt, scuffed white sneakers.

He was the kind of guy who would disappear into a crowd instantly. The kind of guy who would blend.

The kind of guy Jake might have become if fate hadn't chosen a spectacularly odd path for him.

When the guy was satisfied no one was going to jump him, he headed off. Quickly and purposefully through the nearly black forest.

Ordinarily, we might have followed him. Espe-

cially since we assumed he was a Controller, coming up from the Yeerk pool. But Gafinilan was far more important to us now.

Hunkered down to the damp ground, my belly touching pine needles and moss and soil, I moved closer to the cave opening and waited in case there were others. After a few minutes, I sniffed at the entrance. Yes, Gafinilan had been here. I was sort of prepared to go down to the Yeerk pool if we had to. To find the Andalite before he could reveal our secret.

I wasn't prepared for what I found inside the cave.

Nothing. No false panel or trapdoor or secretly coded keypad. Nothing. Just a small, dusty, hollowed-out space in a big rock.

I crawled out of the cave. <Nothing. No entrance. No nothing.>

Ax, perched on one of the sturdy branches that protected the entrance to the cave, said, <Very clever. Obviously where Gafinilan hid his human clothing. For his human morph.>

Of course. Second stupid mistake of the night.

<I've got him,> Tobias called suddenly, from somewhere up above.

I ran. At the edge of the woods, I demorphed and then went owl.

We followed Gafinilan to a neighborhood near the university.

An average neighborhood.

We watched him walk up the driveway to the front door of an average-looking house. A small ranch, like every other house on the block. The name "H. McClellan" in gold letters on the standard-issue black mailbox.

He stopped at the door. Looked around. Then reached into his pocket, took out a set of keys, and let himself in.

We waited. Heard several locks turning and slipping into place.

No lights went on inside the house, even after almost a full four minutes.

<What now?> Tobias said.

<Sneak a peek through a window?>

<No,> Ax said. <Too dangerous. Gafinilan will be ultra careful from this point on. His guard will be up.>

<Okay, guys,> I said. <I'm pretty sure it's time we took this to our fearless leader.>

CHAPTER 7

"Jake, the guy saw me demorph."

Rachel jumped from her seat on a wooden rail. It was early the next morning, before school, which because of some teacher conference was starting late that day. As usual, we were gathered in Cassie's barn. "Great, Marco. Good job," she said sarcastically.

"But," I went on, "he didn't even flinch. Didn't look at me again, didn't talk to me. Didn't ask Ax about me. It was as if he didn't care or something."

"I guess then the question is, why?" Jake said. "Remember how Gonrod almost had a heart attack when he found out there were humans with the morphing power. This guy's *got* to care. Maybe there's something bigger on his mind right now. Something else going on."

"Oh, yeah. Has to be. Like I said before, the guy didn't ask questions," I said. "It didn't make any sense. He didn't ask how Ax knew what was going on with the Rakkam Garroo conflict. Didn't ask about me. Didn't ask how many 'comrades' Ax had. Who 'we' were. Come on. No one's *that* disinterested. That's selective attention. That's calculation."

<He told us the visser was due to arrive momentarily,> Ax added. <As if he knew the visser's habits. As if he were waiting to meet with him.>

<Or maybe to attack him,> Tobias said. <I don't think we should jump to conclusions. We don't know anything about the relationship between Gafinilan and Visser Three.>

I laughed. "Yeah, we do. We know enough. We know there *is* a relationship. That combined with Gafinilan's telling us to get gone. And, of course, his threat to kill us if we didn't leave him and his buddy Mertil alone. In my book, if he's not with us, he's against us."

Jake rubbed the back of his neck. "Let's remember he didn't stay to meet Visser Three. There's always the possibility that these two Andalites could become part of our team. So, we

should keep an eye on this guy. Make sure he's not working for a Yeerk-run company. Or heading off to the Yeerk pool once every three days."

"I'm there," Rachel said.

"I'll go, too." Cassie.

"Fine. Ax, what do you know about Gafinilan?" Jake asked.

<His reputation is flawless,> Ax said simply.

"He almost killed you for insulting his friend," I pointed out. "And he attacked you, a fellow Andalite."

<He is a warrior, not a diplomat,> Ax replied. Perhaps it was me, but he didn't sound one-hundred percent convinced of his argument. <I do not think it unusual for a trained soldier, particularly one stranded far from the home world, in a place under invasion by the enemy, to react as he did.>

"With aggression. Okay, then, what's up with the videotape?" Rachel demanded. "Who took it? How could it have gotten to the show?"

Cassie shrugged. "Lots of possibilities. It could be totally innocent. It might have been taken by some slimy guy out to make some money by selling it to TV. Or to those horrible magazines like the *Star* or *Enquirer*. Or some jerk's idea of a practical joke."

"Or it might have been taken by Gafinilan," Rachel said tightly. "Maybe he's made a deal with the Yeerks. The perfect way to lure the Andalite bandits to certain death."

"But we're still alive," I replied. "So if what you're suggesting is true, I'm positive we would not be having this conversation."

<What if Gafinilan isn't working with the Yeerks?> Tobias said. <What if he had nothing to do with that tape? What if he meant what he said about us leaving him alone? Forgetting about him and Mertil.>

"Too bad," Jake said dryly. "How often do Andalites come to Earth? We can't ignore the fact that Gafinilan and Mertil are holed up in suburbia. Our suburbia. We don't mean them any harm, but we're going to find out as much as we can."

"I take it that means we're going in?" I said. Like I didn't already know.

"Oh, yeah. Only 'we' means you and Ax," Jake said. "If this guy is a traitor, if he's with the Yeerks, we don't want him knowing any more about us than he already does. So, later today Marco as human, which is way too much information already, and Ax as Andalite. He's seen Tobias but we need him to fly surveillance while you two are inside. You are on a formal visit on behalf of your prince, Ax. The rest of us will back you up. Provide firepower if necessary."

I grinned. "Just in case he meant that 'I'll kill

you if you don't leave me alone' thing. Thanks, big guy."

Jake grinned back. "No problem. And when you leave, the rest of us will stay put. Watch where he goes, what he does. See if he contacts the Yeerks. Keep an eye out for Mertil, too." He turned to Rachel and Cassie. "But first, try to catch Mr. H. McClellan before he leaves the house this morning. Tobias, go with them. When they have to get to school, you take over."

Tobias lifted from his perch in the rafters. <Sure, Jake. Meet you in the air, ladies.>

"What am I supposed to do in the meantime?" I said to Jake after all the others had left. "Until Ax and I pay a visit to Batman and Robin?"

Jake gave me a pained smile. "Uh, Marco, I think you've done enough already. You know, the three of you running off to find this Andalite without telling the rest of us. How about taking it easy for a few hours? Maybe say a prayer, or two? We're gonna need it."

CHAPTER 8

I'm not much for prayers and supplication.

Unless, of course, it involves getting a beautiful girl to say "yes" to going out with me. Then, even begging and imploring are options.

<Marco? That you?>

<In the flesh — uh — feathers.>

I'd joined Tobias up above H. McClellan's neighborhood. Above blocks of two- and three-bedroom ranches and split-levels, roofs and gables all cedar shake triangles and trapezoids. Above a collection of backyard pools, bright blue circles and squares, and front yards uniformly rectangular and green. A typically American kind of geometric pattern. Actually kind of cool from this perspective.

<Why aren't you in school with the others?> Tobias asked.

<I'm thinking I really don't want to answer that question. So, what did you find out?>

Tobias coasted into a lazy circle, letting the thermals support him. <Not much. We followed Henry — that's what the "H" stands for — to the university. Seems he's an assistant to some academic type. Some professor who works with particle physics. Whatever that is.>

<Ax will know. What else?>

<Well, except for when the guy went to the bathroom, probably to demorph, we pretty much watched him all morning. Cassie and Rachel got inside. Found out it's the perfect place to demorph. It's one of those private rooms, frosted windows, one stall. Anyway, he sat at his desk, chatted with some coworkers, ate a donut. Then, Rachel and Cassie went to school. I hung around. At about eleven, Henry got a phone call that seemed to shake him up. Next thing I know, he's hightailing it home. Unless he morphed something really small and took off again, I think he's still in there.>

<Or in the greenhouse. I want to get a closer look,> I said.

I glided down, closer to the roof of Henry McClellan's ranch house. Closer to the large greenhouse that was attached to the house itself by a fifteen-foot-long tunnellike extension.

<Be careful, Marco,> Tobias warned. <He's gotta be nervous and definitely paranoid.>

<And probably on the lookout for us, I know, I know.>

<Maybe the call was about Mertil,> Tobias mused as we swooped to about twenty feet above the greenhouse.

<Maybe it was the visser,> I said in a minorly sarcastic voice. <Don't romanticize this.>

Tobias ignored my remark. <There he is,> he said instead. <In Andalite form.>

Gafinilan was barely visible, even to my osprey eyes, beneath the humid, curved glass of the greenhouse and the proliferation of green stuff growing inside.

<According to Ax,> Tobias explained, <gardening is a very cool hobby for Andalites. It's an art, really.>

<Great. I'll be sure to buy him a John Deere riding mower for Christmas. Any sign of Mertil?>

Tobias landed in a huge old oak tree on Mr. Henry McClellan's property. <Not that I can see. Just Gafinilan pruning some leaves. Or doing something with garden shears. He seems pretty focused.>

<Then I'm going in closer.>

<Uh, Marco, I'm not sure that's a great idea. What if he looks up?>

<What if he doesn't?> I countered. <Look, this guy gives me the major willies. I want to know as much as I can before I meet him on his turf.>

<Okay, but . . .> No buts. I was going to get up close and personal with the roof of the greenhouse.

I glided lower, lower, eyes straining to catch every detail I could when . . .

ZZZZZAAAAAPPPPP!

<Ahhhh!>

I hadn't even touched the glass! But a nasty electric jolt sent me toppling over, almost upside down, less than a foot from the glass roof. I righted myself, flapped furiously, desperate not to touch the glass, not even to get as close as I'd come a second before.

<Marco!>

The greenhouse was surrounded by a force field.

Only natural for Gafinilan to go to any lengths to protect himself.

<Marco! Answer me!>

I couldn't. The pain was excruciating. My human mind was numb with shock.

Then I flew. Not toward anything, not even away from anything. The osprey's senses took over and I just flew, up, then down, flapping madly, lost in the pain.

<Marco! What are you doing! Get out of there, now!>

I didn't see the surveillance cameras pop up from the roof of the house.

Until it was too late.

<Look out! He's got a shredder!>

Tobias's cries finally pierced my mindless panic.

I looked back to see Gafinilan's head and weapon-wielding hands poking through a skylight in the flattish roof of the house.

He held a shredder aimed right at me.

<Surrender!> he bellowed in my head.

I didn't answer. Hoping that maybe, just maybe, if I kept quiet, he would think I was only some dumb bird.

Not for the first time, I underestimated him.

Tsseeewww!

He fired!

I saw the flash before I felt the pain.

<Aaaggh!>

One of my talons, completely gone.

<That was a warning shot,> he said.

Some warning.

You can't imagine how disturbing it is to look down and see that one of your body parts is miss-

ing. No matter what form you're in. See the blank space where it used to be. See the blood and gore oozing out of the stump.

<Surrender,> he commanded. <Or die.>

Not much of a choice there.

<Get the others! Find Ax!> I told Tobias privately. <Hurry!>

To Gafinilan: <What do you want me to do?>

He kept the shredder aimed at me. Didn't seem to see Tobias winging off, or didn't care.

<Land in the backyard, beside the greenhouse,> he instructed. <Then, demorph.>

CHAPTER 9

<So, my eyes did not deceive me.> Gafinilan stood there, all three gazillion muscled Andalite pounds of him. <When I first saw you it was night, the light was poor . . . but you are human. Not Andalite.>

I climbed to my feet. No worse for the missing talon. Just a little muddy from rolling around on the ground.

"It looks that way."

Gafinilan poked the shredder at me like a scolding finger.

<Who gave you the morphing technology?> he demanded.

"What difference does that make?"

<The difference between right and wrong,>

Gafinilan shot back. <The Andalite who gave you the power to morph broke the law of *Seerow's Kindness*. He is a criminal.>

"The Andalite who gave me the power to morph is dead," I told him flatly. "And I'm not sure you should be calling anyone else a criminal. You know, let he who is without fault throw the first stone, and all."

<What are you implying, human?>

Suddenly, I was more mad than scared. "I'm not implying anything. I'm saying it outright. You made some kind of deal with Visser Three. I'm not sure of the details yet, or what you stand to get out of it. But this much I do know: Visser Three is a Yeerk. Now, you Andalites are a smart bunch. You tell me what that makes *you*."

SWOOOSH!

My hand flew to my neck. Came away bloody.

Just a little nick. A warning shot.

And then the blade was back at my throat.

<I am no traitor,> Gafinilan said, his thought-speak low and menacing.

<Gafinilan!>

Ax!

Pushing his way through the tall hedges that surrounded McClellan's property. Tail poised, ready to fight.

<If you are a true Andalite,> Ax said, coming to a stop not ten feet away from where we stood,

<you will not harm that human. He is one of us now. A warrior against the Yeerks. Strike him down, and you prove yourself a traitor.>

Gafinilan swung his eye stalks to look at Ax. His main eyes bored into mine.

<You dare to challenge me, little *aristh*?>

<I do,> Ax replied. <The others in the resistance know we are here. It was my prince who sent us to speak with you.>

Gafinilan did not respond. Not right away. He stood perfectly still, regarding us separately, the expression on his face inscrutable.

<I warned you not to approach me,> he said finally. <Your prince insults me by ignoring my command and sending human children.> Slowly, almost tauntingly, he withdrew his tail blade from my throat. <But I will speak with him or I will speak with no one.>

I stepped back. Felt the stinging skin of my neck and said, "Then I guess this conversation is over."

I took a step away from Gafinilan. Then another toward Ax.

<No!>

Slowly, I turned my head and looked back at the big Andalite.

And for a split second, thought I saw a trembling race through his massive body. A slight tremor. Maybe I imagined it.

<No,> he said again, his thought-speak more low and calm. <Please. Come inside.>

<Marco? Ax? We're here. Front and back of the house.>

Jake. Perfect.

"Okay," I said to Gafinilan. "Let's talk."

Gafinilan led Ax and me through a door in the side of the greenhouse's tunnel-like entranceway. From there, we entered the house itself through a very typical back door, screen and all.

And stepped into a kitchen straight out of *Martha Stewart Living* or *House Beautiful* or *Architectural Digest.* One of those lifestyle magazines my stepmother is always reading.

<Your home is an accurate and attractive example of a human suburban dwelling,> Ax said formally.

<I appreciate your assessment, Aximili,> Gafinilan replied, just as formally. <It has been difficult, learning the many details of human culture. But it is important for Mertil and me to remain as inconspicuous as possible by hiding in plain sight. Although I must admit the relative lowness of this roof is at times disconcerting. Nothing like living under the open sky.>

"That's a ranch house for you," I said. "Next time, go for a Cape Cod, at least. Or skylights in every room, not just the kitchen."

Gafinilan chose to ignore my remark. He led us

through the kitchen, a veritable shrine to modern domestic technology. A Sub-Zero fridge. Microwave. Viking cooktop and oven. State-of-the-art Bosch dishwasher. Cuisinart. KitchenAid mixer. And everything was sparkling clean. Nora would have been in heaven. Okay. Maybe I've been spending too much time watching that kitchen show on the Food Network.

"Yeah, great kitchen, Gafinilan," I said. "But it looks like it's never been used. No dirty dishes in the sink, no dustpan against the wall, no soaking wet dish towels thrown on a counter. No way anyone's going to believe two guys live here."

Gafinilan focused his main eyes on me. <Two "guys" do not live here,> he said. <At least as far as other humans are concerned. This house belongs only to a Henry McClellan and he resides alone. He lives quietly. He spends most of his time at his office at the university. He does not have friends. He is what humans call a "loner.">

Well, that answered that question. Gafinilan led us through several other rooms in the house, each equally pristine, each obviously unused. I mean, white carpeting? Pink silk upholstery? For two guys with muddy hooves and no ability to sit?

Clearly, Mertil and Gafinilan actually lived somewhere else in the house.

The only disturbingly out-of-place items in the otherwise perfect house were a few pieces of

artwork, obviously bought at some starving artist sale set up along a highway. You know, paintings on black velvet, sold from the trunk of an old Cadillac. There were the requisite seascapes and even a sad-eyed clown.

Before I could ask where the crying Elvis was hung, Gafinilan led us back to the kitchen. On the far wall was a keypad. The Andalite's massive shoulders blocked our view of it as he punched in the code. A concealed door to the left of the pad slid open.

<Please. These are our private quarters.>

In semiprivate thought-speak, Ax let Jake know our position. That we were entering a concealed part of the house. That he and the others should be ready to come at our call.

Then Ax and I stepped forward. I whistled. It was a mini Andalite home-away-from-home.

<Mertil and I were fortunate to have salvaged many things after the crash,> Gafinilan explained. <Most important, a good power supply and a force field generator. The latter is particularly necessary for our survival.>

I smiled wryly. "You don't say."

Computer stations. More than half a dozen of them. Each screen running a different program, none of which looked familiar to me at first glance.

Several large-screen TVs. Each on and tuned to a different news program. Everything from

Hollywood Style Report to CNN to the Bloomberg Report.

The floor was covered in lush, well-tended grass. No chairs, but a long, fairly high table on which lay various handheld weapons.

The walls were painted a creamy color. The ceiling, sky-blue. There seemed to be no other rooms beyond or off this large one. There might have been, of course. There might have been another secret sliding panel. There probably was.

Because we did not see Mertil.

CHAPTER 10

<War Prince Gafinilan, I would like to understand why you seem to have no interest in joining our fight against Yeerk domination.>

And things had been going so well.

But instead of watching Ax's head roll across the grassy floor, I watched the expression in Gafinilan's face mutate from fury to despair to a typical Andalite inscrutability. All in the space of a few seconds.

<Very well, young Aximili,> he said, slouching slightly into a more relaxed, less angry pose. <Perhaps you will find my story an unlikely one, but it is true. And it is mine. As I have told you,> he went on, <at one time, not so long ago, I was engaged in the war against the Yeerks. Assigned

to the Dome ship's forces, as was your esteemed brother, Elfangor.>

<Yes.>

<Mertil and I were fighter pilots. We came up through the academy together and each earned a reputation for excellence and bravery. However, no one is immune to the vagaries of war. During the battle with the Blade ship, the battle that destroyed the Dome ship, my fighter was hit and the main engine was destroyed. Almost immediately I lost control and slammed into Mertil's already damaged fighter. Our wings somehow locked and, as one, the ships spiraled to the ground. I was sure we would both be killed.>

He paused, then after a few tense moments, he continued.

<Instead, we became two more living casualities of war. For some reason, we both survived. Spent several excruciating months hiding in the woods, dodging prying eyes, until I was able to acquire a human morph and venture into the world. You see, I only sustained minor injuries. A few burns, easily healed broken ribs. Mertil, however, was more seriously hurt. In time, he recovered from his other injuries. But his tail — it was severed. And because of his inability to utilize the morphing technology, there was nothing that could be done. He will never be restored to his normal self. And now, I am no longer a warrior in

the service of the Andalite world. I am Mertil's protector and friend. After all,> he added, his thought-speak dark, <if I had been able to maintain control of my plane, Mertil might not have suffered as he has.>

<Terrible,> Ax said. There was a trace of sympathy in his thought-speak. Just a trace. <Mertil was deprived a hero's death and forced to live out the rest of his days as a *vecol*.>

<I am happy Mertil is alive,> Gafinilan countered.

I believed him.

"So, where is he?" I asked. "I'd like to meet him."

<Impossible!> Ax.

<No!> Gafinilan.

"Oookay. So, can I ask why?"

"It is unthinkable to intrude upon the isolation of a *vecol*,> Ax explained. <His isolation is the only dignity he has.>

"Well, it's not like I'm going to point and laugh or anything," I said. "I can't even say 'hey' to the guy?"

No answer, from either Andalite.

Maybe I should have kept my mouth shut. Probably. But there are some topics I just can't let alone.

I faked a laugh. "You Andalites need some serious attitude adjustment when it comes to the differently abled."

<We have our ways,> Ax said simply.

<Aximili!> Gafinilan said heartily. Changing the subject. <Will you honor me by sharing some *illsipar* root?>

Here's the thing. When Ax is in human morph he can't get enough of cinnamon buns. I mean, it's frightening. Well, I saw that same crazed look flit across his normally expressionless Andalite face. The look that says, "Give it to me now or I will be forced to hurt you."

<Thank you,> he said carefully. <I have not had *illsipar* root since leaving the home world.>

Gafinilan clomped through the back door and led us into the main section of the greenhouse.

<You are an expert gardener, Gafinilan,> Ax said.

<I have been studying the art of botanical cultivation since my youth. It has been a challenge, but a rewarding one, to learn about the care and nurturing of Earth plants.>

I know next to nothing about green things, but even I could see this Andalite had a green thumb. As it were. At least ten varieties of flowers, in pots and in orderly beds on the ground. Two kinds of roses, purple peonies, orange daylilies — Gafinilan had been nice enough to pro-

vide clearly labeled signs for the ignorant. Bushes and shrubs, leaves glossy green, some flowering. Several slim potted trees. Even a small section of Japanese rock garden, complete with neatly raked gravel.

<I have grown the *illsipar* from seeds from my home world garden,> Gafinilan explained. In his oddly huge hand, he held five or six stalks of what looked a lot like scallions. Except pinkish. <It is a hearty plant and grows well here.>

I watched, almost fascinated, as both Andalites placed several stalks of the root on the ground and then proceeded to eat them in the normal Andalite fashion. Crushing the plant beneath their hooves and absorbing its nutrients.

Then the almost-fascination ended. It seemed the Andalites had forgotten I was there. So I took a closer look at some of the more exotic-looking stuff Gafinilan was cultivating. Strolled down one narrow aisle and up the next, each littered with bags of potting soil, trowels, watering cans, and cacti in flattish bowls.

"Bzzzzz!"

What the . . .

I smacked the air with my hand. Stupid bee.

"Bzzzzz!"

Another one! Smack!

But I was wasting my time. The bees weren't interested in me. They were interested in the sweet and colorful flowers that filled the greenhouse.

Of course. Gafinilan relied on the bees to help fertilize his plants.

Quickly, I checked to see if Ax and his host were still absorbed in the *illsipar* ritual. They were.

Then checked out the greenhouse for a hive. None.

Checked my brain to see if I know anything about honeybees. Like, do they sting? Nothing there.

But I was going to acquire a honeybee regardless. If the bees were coming from and returning to a hive somewhere outside the greenhouse — without getting zapped by the force field — that meant they knew a safe way in and out.

Just what I needed.

I stood still. Hoped I smelled my sweetest. And . . .

"Bzzzzz!"

Got it! Held the bee loosely in my fist and hoped I acquired it.

<Thank you for the excellent *illsipar* root.>

Ax! Still clutching the bee, I peeked around a potted plant to see the two Andalites had finished their snack.

<You are welcome,> Gafinilan answered, one stalk eye pointed my way.

I smiled.

<Perhaps now your prince will honor me with a visit?> Gafinilan said. <Now that you see I mean no harm. Will you tell him that I invite him to enjoy some of this home world specialty?>

<I must explain . . .>

"Yes, of course," I said, cutting Ax off. Hoping he'd keep quiet. "We'll extend your invitation."

Ax looked back at me, slightly puzzled. I grinned crazily.

The stupid bee had stung me!

Ow! I opened my fist, out of sight, and tossed the bee to the ground.

Then I came forward to join the other two.

<Excellent.> Suddenly, Gafinilan was all conviviality, the host with the most. <I look forward to your return and to meeting your prince!>

CHAPTER 11

Ax's prince and my best friend was not going to pay a visit to Gafinilan before I did a little further investigation on my own.

But I didn't tell him that.

We met at the mall, Ax, in his human morph, and I strolling in together, stopping here and there, looking like a couple of normal guys hanging out at the mall.

Jake on his own. Browsing through the Nike store, pretending to still be interested in something as harmless and normal as sports.

Tobias with Rachel. She, carrying a bag from Express and one from Bebe. He, looking slightly awkward and out of place.

Finally, Cassie. In a pair of jeans that actually fit.

Accidentally on purpose, we hooked up in the food court. Ax wanted to buy a box of cinnamon buns. Jake thought a Pepsi sounded good. What do you know?

We gathered at an empty table and while Ax stuffed his face and I pretended to flip through a comic book I pulled out of my back pocket, we told the others what had gone down.

"You know you took a huge — and I'll add, too, stupid — risk, Marco," Jake said, keeping his voice low and his expression bland.

"Yeah, well, we got what we wanted," I said. "We got inside. And we got to confirm that Gafinilan is a bit of a loose cannon."

"Yes," Ax agreed. Though it was hard to take him seriously with frosting on his chin. "His mood does not seem perfectly stable. Bul. But he is a fine gardener. And he has created an impressive human cover."

"Yeah, down to the patterned paper towels," I muttered, tossing the comic book on the table. "The place is too perfect."

Rachel leaned in to the conversation. "Sounds like he's overcompensating. Trying too hard. It's understandable. He's got to be scared."

"Of who?" Tobias asked. "Us or the Yeerks?"

Jake slurped down the rest of his soda. "He

wants to meet Ax's prince. I say we pay him a visit."

"Not a good idea, man. Look, I'm getting a very bad feeling about this guy. This situation. I'm not reading clear motives. I say we wait before sending you in."

Jake shrugged. "For what? For the visser to grab him? For Gafinilan to tell the visser there's at least one human 'Andalite bandit'?"

"It's risky," Cassie added. "Marco's right."

"We take precautions, per usual. I go in with cover."

Jake stood. "Gotta get home. My mom's cooking one of my favorites tonight for dinner. If I'm late, she'll wonder."

"I'll walk out with you," Cassie said.

"Let's plan on my meeting Gafinilan as soon as possible," Jake said. "Maybe tomorrow night."

"I'm out of here, too." Tobias stood and twitched his arms. "This place weirds me out. Ax-man? You coming?"

Ax patted his stomach. "Yes, Tobias. I believe I am full for the moment." He stood and gathered up the shredded remains of the Cinnabon box.

It was me and Rachel, alone.

I puffed out my chest and smiled. "Any particular reason you wanted to be alone with me, Rachel?"

"Yeah. So I could watch you act stupid. The usual." She leaned back in her seat. "I mean it, Marco. I'm not in the mood."

I put my hands up, conceding defeat.

"Okay, okay. So . . . ?"

"A lot of times you're a major cynical freak, you know?"

I barked a laugh. "Uh, thanks. I guess."

"But you're also the best at knowing when something genuinely stinks. I can block out your lame jokes but I can't ignore your paranoid instincts."

"Gee, thanks, again," I said.

Rachel frowned. "I mean it. Look, you're not letting Jake meet Gafinilan before you go back there yourself. Don't bother to deny it. You have a plan. I want to know what it is."

Quickly, casually, I glanced around. "Why? So you can tell your Bird-boyfriend and screw me up with Jake?"

"No, you moron," Rachel hissed. "So I can go with you. You'll need someone to cover your butt."

"See! I knew you cared."

WHAM!

And that's when Rachel's foot connected squarely with my shin.

CHAPTER 12

There wouldn't be time to do my bee morph before my "mission." So I spent a few minutes on the Internet, hoping to discover some pertinent facts about the bee's capabilities and weaknesses. Something that might help me know what to expect when the honeybee brain kicked in.

And I learned something that scared the tar out of me: that honeybees, like ants, are social insects. Just not to the same extent as ants. But they function as part of a greater whole. Not individuals. Machinelike in their dedication to the survival of the colony. Devoted one hundred and fifty percent to the hive.

Now you know where the saying "busy as a bee" came from.

This did not make me happy. Being an ant had been one of the most frightening experiences of my otherwise already-bizarre life.

I'd lost myself, going ant. So had Jake and the others. There had been no sense of self. Of individuality. Most people can't even imagine what losing that part of you feels like. It's one hundred times more intense than your worst nightmare.

I took a deep breath. I would have to avoid the actual hive if at all possible.

I looked at my watch. Time flies when you're scared peeless.

We met way too early in the morning. Rachel used her bald eagle morph and I went osprey. And we flew to Henry McClellan's house.

<Now what?> she asked.

<Land and survey.>

We did. Before a full three minutes had passed, we spotted a honeybee.

And it was headed toward the greenhouse.

Perfect. Maybe I wouldn't need to find the colony after all.

<What is it doing?> Rachel said.

<I don't know. Just pay attention.>

Which wasn't very easy. The bee zipped along erratically. Up, then down. To the right, then down again. Left! Up! Slanting on a diagonal! Reversing direction, backtracking.

Then, in a final show of acrobatic skill, slipping effortlessly through a tiny hole in a panel of glass.

<Okay, Marco,> Rachel said. <There's your way in.>

<Cripes. I'll never make it through that nuclear obstacle course without getting fried.>

<Not unless you follow another bee,> Rachel pointed out. <I mean, really tailgate. Which means we need the hive.>

She was right. Adopting the buddy system with a honeybee was my safest — not to mention only — chance of getting inside.

We found the hive carefully hidden in a small cluster of trees at the far end of Henry McClellan's backyard.

<Where'd Gafinilan get the money for this place?> I grumbled. <The yard's got to be, like, three acres.>

<Lotto?> Rachel landed on a branch of the live oak next to the partially rotted-out old tree that housed the resident honeybee community. <I'll cover you while you demorph. After you morph, I'll keep an eye on you as you get closer to the house. Anything goes wrong in there, Marco, you'd better call me,> she warned. <No being a hero.>

<No danger of that,> I muttered.

I landed at the foot of Rachel's tree. Quickly demorphed and scurried over to stand just below the hive. Cut down on postmorph travel.

None of us enjoy morphing anything really small. Particularly insects. Particularly ants, which are so, so not human. Honeybees are a lot cuter than ants. All fuzzy and stuff. Maybe this means they are less driven and simpleminded and violent. Right?

Now or never. I crouched to minimize the insane fall that would come as I shrank down to the size of a Gummy Bear. And I held the image of the honeybee in my mind.

Morphing is not logical or orderly. It does not proceed in a preordained pattern. It is not predictable.

This time, the first bit of me to go was the part of my torso that became the bee's thorax. Marco to about midway down my chest. Bee thorax. Marco below. Ugh.

Have I mentioned that the honeybee has an exoskeleton? Which precludes the need for an internal skeleton. So I'm pretty sure I was mostly ribless and partially spineless at the moment.

<That is so nauseating,> Rachel remarked helpfully.

I chose not to respond.

Chitin. That's what the exoskeleton is made

of, a hard substance that protects the internal organs and also keeps them from drying out.

Fliip. Fliip.

Two sets of flat, thin wings sprang from the bee's thorax. Membranes, really, lined with veins, the set in front, larger. Together, using a propeller-like twisting motion, the two sets allowed the honeybee to fly.

Poofpoofpoof . . .

Hundreds, thousands of little hairs sprouted from all over my body.

<Okay, that's a lot better,> Rachel noted.

Also on the thorax, three pairs of segmented legs. When the morph was complete I would be able to walk and even use the frontmost legs to clean my antennae.

Next to show up were the antennae. Segmented and coated with tiny hairs. Super-important sensory organs. Sensitive to touch and odor. Attached directly to the brain.

Cool. I could move the antennae because each was set in a socket on my head.

Huh? Okay, human head was rapidly becoming the kind of triangular head of the bee.

My human mouth, suddenly sealed.

My chin, splitting down the cleft.

Shloop!

And shooting out of that vertical mouth, a

proboscis. A long and hairy tongue that would allow the bee to drink liquids.

Mandibles, a pair on either side of my head. Kind of like pliers. Useful for eating pollen and manipulating wax and snatching enemies.

Okay, gross. I was blind, my human eyes gone.

Then: Pop! Pop! Popopopopop!

Vision. Thousands of teeny lenses showing me thousands of pieces of the world. All combining to make one huge-faceted mosaic or gridlike picture.

The bee couldn't distinguish color as well as a human. That red birdhouse I'd spotted before morphing — not red to the bee.

But boy, could I see movement! Forms were not as clear or obvious as was the fluttering of flowers on their stems or the flitting of a butterfly from leaf to leaf.

Pop! Pop! Pop!

Three more eyes, small, shot out above my compound eyes. They couldn't really distinguish anything, not movement or form. But the eyes did seem to detect light.

And here came the abdomen.

Oh, lucky me. I was a female. How did I know this? Because my abdomen was slimmer than the rounder abdomen of the male drone, for one.

But mostly because I had a stinger. It was about one eighth of an inch long and at the end of my abdomen. Kind of worked like a hypodermic needle. Except the tip was barbed so that it would stick into the skin of the honeybee's victim. And it shot poison, not some vitamin formula.

Nice to have a weapon. But don't use it, Marco, the human brain in me reminded. If I stung an enemy, part of the stinger would remain in the enemy after I'd broken free. And I would die. Just like the bee I'd acquired. The bee who'd stung me.

But as the morph came to completion, I wasn't thinking about cause and effect — sting and die. Thinking about cause and effect — that was a human brain thing to do.

And right then, I was all honeybee. All armored flying insect with a vital mission — to work and work and work for the hive. For the queen.

The hive! I had to get to the hive!

CHAPTER 13

I shot up from the ground.

<Marco! Get a grip!> A harsh sound. Meaningless to the bee. <You're not supposed to go in the hive!>

I landed on the lip of the hollowed section of the dead tree. Was met by a guard bee, another worker, like myself. I did not smell like the enemy. So round and round in circles, first this way, then that, the other bee twirled on its three sets of legs. Flicking its wings, my comrade told me the location of a new source of food for the hive.

All for the hive!

I would go and gather . . .

<Marco! What are you doing?>

What . . . man. My brain finally shook itself back into place. What *was* I doing?

I left my hive-mate and lifted off. Zoomed out and over to Rachel, still perched in the next tree in eagle morph.

<What's wrong with you?> she snapped. <It's a stupid honeybee!>

<Sorry. But I'm not sure I'd call the bee stupid. You need individuality and sentience to be stupid, don't you? As compared to smart or silly or whatever?>

<I guess,> Rachel conceded.

<Anyway, it's not nearly as bad as being an ant. You know how ants are just programmed parts of a whole? It's kind of like that, only not so aggressive. It's sort of like I'm part of a big farm family. All for one and one for all while we bring in the crop and feed the next generation and pay homage to the queen. That's what Communism is all about,> I mused. <I mean, Castro's like a king when you think about it.>

<Yeah, well, Comrade Marco, just be sure you maintain control, okay?>

<Yeah. Look, there's a couple of bees flying out of the hive. Might as well follow them and hope for the best.>

<I'm on you.>

I zipped off after the two bees. One zoomed off the property. The other seemed headed for the greenhouse.

So far, on a fairly straight path.

ZZZZZZZZ!

Not another bee. Not my bee. Another bug.

Whoosh!

It dropped straight down in front of me! Went right for the bee I was following!

What the heck was it?

Through what seemed like thousands of tiny TV screens I could see an insect larger than me, maybe twice my size. Its legs seemed to be covered in spines or spikes. Its nose looked like a big fat needle.

<Marco! You'd better look out!> Rachel called.

And then the monster insect hit the bee. Hard. Wrapped its horrible legs around it, capturing the smaller insect in a spiny, iron maiden-like prison.

Like one gigantic mutant insect they flew. The bee struggled but to no effect.

And then the big bandit stabbed the bee with its needle-nose. Had to be sucking the life from the bee, because when the big insect released the carcass it was withered and dry.

A terrible close call. But the killer insect had flown out of sight . . .

<Marco! He's coming back for you!>

ZZZZZZZZZZZ!

<He's about a foot behind you, maybe six inches up. I'll try to get him but . . .>

<Ahhhhh!>

I felt one of his barbed legs pierce my abdomen.

No no no no!

A second leg impaled me from the other side.

I was a skewered snack for a seriously unattractive insect.

At least it would be quick. How long had it taken this thing to suck the life out of the other bee?

I felt the proboscis against my back. The very tip of the deadly sucking needle.

WHOOOOSSSHHH!

A massive gust of wind sent me swirling, then falling toward the ground.

Falling, but not dead.

I tried to move my wings, get control. But they were still pinned against my body by the grip of the demon on my back.

Thump!

I hit the ground. Stunned but alive.

<Marco!> Rachel cried. <Are you okay?>

<I'm alive,> I said. <But not okay. The thing's still got me!>

<Oh, you're fine,> she said. <I got him. Tore him right in half. Sorry I let you fall.>

<You're forgiven. Just get me the heck out of here, will you?>

A bald eagle dive-bombing bugs in the back-yard? Not too odd.

With massive eagle claws, Rachel grabbed me and what was left of the killer. We flew into the dense trees back by the hive where, one at a time, we demorphed and remorphed. Got ready to try this insane thing again.

This time, Rachel was on the lookout for winged hijackers.

After about ten minutes, another few bees headed off toward Gafinilan's greenhouse. I followed.

<I see the force field,> I called out.

<Be careful, Marco.>

Let me tell you I more than realized I could definitely be fried in the force field, but it was a spectacular thing to actually see. A color I'd never seen as a human. Unbelievable. Indescribable. Something I later learned was called "bee-purple." It's the color between yellow and ultra-violet on the spectrum. Too intense for the human eye to see.

Too bad. Because it was intense. And running right through it, easily marked, was a curving tunnel. Actually quite wide for a bee. And the tunnel led ultimately to a small hole in a glass panel of the greenhouse's back wall.

Cake. A piece of cake.

<I'm almost in,> I called to Rachel.

<Uh, Marco? Heads up. Gafinilan just came into the greenhouse.>

Too late. Had to take the chance. I slipped in behind another honeybee. Frighteningly close to Gafinilan, who was peering intently at one of his plant labels, holding it close to his two main eyes.

Suddenly, he swiveled his eye stalks toward us. Noted our appearance. And swiveled them back to his own business.

<I'm okay so far,> I said. <Heading into the house.>

I'd noted on my first visit that Gafinilan hadn't closed the back door of the house, the one that connected the kitchen to the greenhouse. Had counted on his not doing so again.

Luck was with me.

So far, anyway.

I zipped through the open door.

Flew through every room in the house. The immaculately kept living room. Unused dining room. Pristine kitchen.

And I used the honeybee's eyes and antennae to try to pick up more information.

I smelled the flowers, plants, and potting soil from the greenhouse. The chocolate and raisins of the cookies Gafinilan had stacked inside sev-

eral glass Mason jars. A strong, disinfectant smell in the bathroom. Mr. Clean or Top Job or Comet.

Throughout the house, in every room, Gafinilan's distinctive, not unpleasant odor.

But there was one thing I distinctly did not see or smell or sense in any way.

<What's in there?> Rachel asked.

<I'll tell you what's *not* in here,> I said. <And what hasn't been here for a long time. Mertil.>

CHAPTER 14

"I don't get it. Where is Mertil?" Jake said. But only after he stopped telling me he was getting really ticked at me and this whole Gafinilan thing. After he stopped glaring at Rachel. After he admitted the information about the missing Andalite was valuable. We were all in Cassie's barn. And things were getting consistently more confusing. "Did he ever exist? Was the guy on the video a fake?"

<Prince Jake, I can confirm there was a Mertil-Iscar-Elmand at the Andalite Academy. And that a fighter pilot by the same name won much honor afterward.> Ax paused thoughtfully. <Of course, I did not know he was morph incapable. I was un-

der the impression the academy did not admit *vecols*.>

"Yeah," I snapped, "you hate when your hero turns out to be a cripple. That's pretty crappy."

"Back to the point," Jake said tightly. "Which is, what do we do about Gafinilan?"

Rachel sprawled on a stack of hay bales. "He doesn't want to hurt us. Not yet, anyway. But he doesn't want to help us, either. He says he wants us to leave him alone, but then he asks to meet Jake. Doesn't make sense."

<I don't think the guy knows what he wants . . .>

<Yes, Tobias. Yes, he does,> Ax said excitedly. <*Illsipar* root. Why didn't I see before!>

I shook my head. "See what?"

<Gafinilan offered me *illsipar* root,> Ax explained. <It is a mild intoxicant, taken in a manner somewhat like humans take tea or coffee each morning.>

"Okay, but . . ."

<*Illsipar* root has a medicinal use, as well. In great quantities, it eases the pain of *Soola's* Disease. This is a genetically programmed disease. It causes increasing pain in the joints as well as the muscles, extreme at the end. In some, it causes progressive blindness. It strikes in the prime of life and is always fatal.>

"Okay," Jake said. "I still don't understand what this disease has to do with us."

"And I don't understand," Rachel began, "why, if Gafinilan has the disease, he can't cure himself by morphing. Oh. Wait. Yes I do. His own DNA still has the disease. It's like he's trapped."

Ax inclined his head. <Exactly. The only cure is to acquire, then morph, another Andalite. One without the defective gene that predisposes toward the disease. In other words, the victim of *Soola's* Disease must abandon his imperfect body. He must become a *nothlit.*>

Tobias looked at Ax with his intensely fierce hawk's eyes. <Sounds reasonable.>

<No. In Andalite society, choosing to become a *nothlit* in such a situation or for such a purpose is considered an act of cowardice. Morally wrong. Despicable.>

"If Gafinilan is sick, why haven't we seen signs of his being in pain? And if acquiring another Andalite is what Gafinilan intends," Cassie mused, "why wouldn't he just have acquired Ax?"

Ax had an answer for that, too. <Gafinilan is an adult with an impressive warrior's physique. He would never choose to adopt the body of a mere youth. He would waste years waiting for the new young body to grow to its maximum poten-

tial. Besides, I would never give my permission for such an act. As for Gafinilan's exhibiting no signs of pain in public, that is only seemly. A warrior is trained not to show signs of physical weakness or mental strain.> Ax paused. <But the pain escalates the nearer death approaches, it is unlikely he will be able to completely hide his agony.>

"So, you think Gafinilan was — or is, still — hoping to acquire Visser Three's Andalite . . ." I stopped. "Well, that wouldn't be *too* difficult or anything."

"No. I'm pretty sure he wants me," Jake said suddenly. "At least, he wants who he thinks I am. A healthy adult Andalite."

"But Ax said to become the *nothlit* is an act of cowardice," Cassie pointed out. "You think Gafinilan is a coward? I don't. Not the way he disregards Andalite custom to care for Mertil."

"Nice, Cassie," I snapped. "At the very least the guy's a liar. And he's big on keeping secrets. I don't trust him as far as I can throw him. Which is about one tenth of an inch. Maybe."

"I have to agree," Rachel added. "Gafinilan is in a bad place. If he's after an Andalite body, who knows what he'll do when — if — he finds out Jake is human."

"Same thing he did to Mertil," I muttered. "I'm thinking it's not Mertil's happiness he's after. I'm thinking he probably made that tape of his buddy himself. Put it out there to lure any other Andalites who might just be hanging around planet Earth. Then when Mertil did his part, Gafinilan put him out of his misery. The incredible disappearing Andalite."

"Pretty harsh, Marco." Cassie.

<But it could very well be the truth,> Ax said solemnly. <As much as it pains me to acknowledge the possibility of such behavior on the part of a fellow Andalite.>

<Loyalty,> Tobias said quietly, enigmatically, <is all there is.>

"Ax?" It was Cassie, beginning to sound excited. "What about the morphing cube? The Escafil Device? Could we use that on Mertil? Give him the power to morph?"

"What difference would that make if he's dead?" Rachel said darkly.

Ax hesitated. <It is likely that Mertil is allergic to, or has some disease or disorder which makes his body reject the morphing technology. In which case, what good is our forcing it upon him?>

Jake stood abruptly. "Look, we're not getting any closer to the truth by sitting around speculating. Is Mertil dead or alive? Is Gafinilan a bad guy or isn't he? Only way to know is to get to him. And hope we're the first ones there."

CHAPTER 15

So we went. I coached Tobias, Rachel, Cassie, and Ax on what to expect when they morphed the honeybee. Warned them about clutching the bee too tight when they acquired it. Warned them also about what Cassie told me was a robber fly, the demon insect who'd tried to make me into a bee smoothie.

The plan was for the five of us to sneak onto McClellan/Gafinilan's property. Acquire a bee from the resident hive. And fly through the force field and into Gafinilan's greenhouse.

When we were in place, Jake would ring the front doorbell. I'd slip into the house and stick with Gafinilan and Jake. The others would hang back until — if — we got in trouble and needed major backup.

And trouble could come from Gafinilan or the Yeerks. First, we had to make certain the house wasn't being watched before Jake went up the driveway. That meant concentrated surveillance.

Beyond getting Jake inside to talk to the big Andalite, our plan was vague. Mostly contingent on Gafinilan's actions.

When we were in morph, and safely in the greenhouse, I gave Jake the okay.

A moment later, he rang the front doorbell.

<Wish us luck, kids,> I said.

Gafinilan put down the bottle of liquid fertilizer he was preparing and headed into the house through the back door. I followed him. Close but not close enough to arouse suspicion and be swatted to death.

Once in the living room, Gafinilan morphed to Henry McClellan. Then walked to the front door. Opened it as far as the chain lock would allow.

"Yes?" he said, keeping his body almost entirely behind the door, allowing only part of his face to show.

"Gafinilan?" Jake kept his voice low.

"No. No, my name is Henry McClellan."

Gafinilan began to close the door.

"I know," Jake said quickly. "That's your human name. Aximili told me. I'm Jake."

Slowly, the door closed. Gafinilan undid the chain. Opened the door again. Stepped back.

"Come inside," he said.

Jake did. Gafinilan relocked the door behind him.

"You are Aximili's prince?"

"Yes," Jake answered.

The Andalite's human morph relaxed slightly. I could hear it in his voice.

"I am pleased that you have accepted the invitation to meet with me," he said. "Perhaps it would be better if we spoke in surroundings more comfortable to both of us. Please, follow me."

Gafinilan led Jake through the sparkling kitchen and into his private quarters. He stepped aside to allow Jake to enter first.

"Very nice," Jake said.

The Andalite followed and programmed the door shut behind them. Behind me, too.

The three of us were alone. Cut off from the others, waiting in the greenhouse.

"As I told young Aximili," Gafinilan said, conversationally, "Mertil and I were fortunate to have salvaged much from the wreckage of our fighters. Tell me, was there much to be salvaged of the Dome ship? Or did Earth's ocean destroy it all?"

Whoa. Ax had already told Gafinilan he was the only survivor. Except for Gafinilan and Mertil. What was Gafinilan up to?

Jake looked steadily at Henry McClellan. "The Dome ship was almost completely destroyed," he answered. Noncommittally.

"Yes, yes." Henry's eyes darted around the room. Then he looked back to Jake. "Jake. It is a good name. Is it a shortened version of something else, like 'Ax' for Aximili?"

"It's just what people call me."

Jake was giving the guy nothing.

Gafinilan spoke loudly. With false heartiness. "Please, make yourself comfortable. As will I."

He stepped toward the center of the grassy room. Began to demorph.

<Why haven't you demorphed?> he asked when he'd finished.

Jake smiled. "I prefer to speak with you in this form."

<But you insult a fellow Andalite by not revealing your true self,> Gafinilan coaxed. His own eyes smiling the way Andalites do.

"My true physical self is irrelevant."

<Prince Jake.> Gafinilan's voice was forceful now, almost threatening. <I insist that you demorph from this ridiculous morph.>

"After you explain what you really want from me," Jake countered.

<Enough!> Gafinilan took a step toward Jake, tail blade raised high, arched forward over his back.

And then he stumbled, on nothing. Groaned. Closed all four eyes.

No doubt about it. The guy was in pain.

Ax was right. *Soola's* Disease. Or something else pretty serious and getting worse.

Jake started to move forward. Instinctively, to help.

<No!> I said. <Wait. Let him tell us what we need to know.>

He stopped himself. Checked the impulse. Waited.

"Gafinilan . . ."

The Andalite opened his eyes, the main ones first. Regained his composure.

<No,> he said, his voice hard but low. <There will be no more talk.>

He turned away from Jake. Stepped slowly to the table of weapons. Picked up a shredder.

Turned and pointed it at Jake.

<Now you will do as I say.>

CHAPTER 16

<We've got a problem,> I called out to the others. <We need reinforcements in here. Now!>

<What will it be, Prince Jake?> Gafinilan said. <If you think I will show you mercy because you appear as a child, you are mistaken.>

Jake stood perfectly still. "What if I am a child?" he said calmly. As if a shredder were not leveled a few feet from his face.

<Backup on the way, Jake,> I said.

Gafinilan's tail twitched. <You bore me with this game! For an Andalite warrior, you are not particularly clever.>

"Hrrooooaaaarrr!!"

From the direction of the greenhouse came

the menacing roar of a grizzly. The lonely howl of a wolf. The bloodcurdling screech of a raptor.

Gafinilan jerked toward the sounds.

And then there was one loud BABOOM! as Rachel crashed through one of the walls like a baseball crashing through a window. But making a lot more mess.

Cassie, Ax, and Tobias followed almost daintily through the rubble.

"I'm sorry we bore you, Gafinilan," Jake said calmly. "But we're bored, too. Tired of your evasions and half-truths. So if it's okay with you, this is the moment of reckoning. Time to come clean."

<Four warriors against one?> Gafinilan blustered.

"Five, if I morph," I said, having demorphed behind the weapons table, walking around to face our host. "Six if Jake does."

"But we're not here to fight, Gafinilan," Jake said. "Just to get some information."

Gafinilan's two stalk eyes swiveled madly for a second. Then a look of shocked understanding came to them. <You, all of you — you are the Andalite bandits Visser Three fears. Are all of you but Aximili — human?>

"Yes," Jake said. He shot a glance at Tobias. "More or less. We were enlisted by Prince Elfangor to fight the Yeerks."

<You see,> Ax said matter-of-factly, <there is no adult Andalite for you to acquire so that you may escape *Soola's* Disease.>

<What!> Gafinilan roared, pointing his shredder at Ax. <How dare you make such an accusation! I am a warrior. Never in a galaxy's age would I disgrace myself by acting with such base and selfish cowardice.>

Silence. Gafinilan's hand began to shake and he lowered the shredder. And then Tobias spoke.

<You know, in the Andalite world, it might be considered a moral failing or a crime against personal honor or something to seek to cure yourself in any way you can. But not here. Not on Earth.>

<He's right,> Cassie added quickly. <We don't judge or condemn people who seek health through legitimate paths. We . . .>

Gafinilan raised the shredder again. <You don't understand at all!> he cried, despairingly. <Nobody understands.>

"Why don't you explain," Jake suggested quietly.

There was a moment of silence. A moment during which I thought it pretty likely Gafinilan would do something desperate. Tension radiated from every inch of him. And then he shuddered, like he'd made a decision, and the tension was replaced by what looked and felt a lot like exhaustion.

He lowered the shredder again and spoke.

<It is true. I have *Soola's* Disease. But what I have done I have not done for myself. I have done all for Mertil.>

<Obviously, Mertil is not morph capable,> Ax said. <I do not understand.>

The ghost of a small, self-mocking smile appeared in Gafinilan's main eyes. <You see? Nobody understands. I suppose there is no reason to keep the truth from you,> he conceded. <Some human, some meddlesome, possibly innocent human stumbled upon Mertil feeding. Visser Three saw the tape — whether on television or in some other way, I do not know. But it was enough. Mertil was seized by the Yeerks. Only then did the visser discover that Mertil was a *vecol*.> Gafinilan's voice tightened. <Of course, the Yeerks have no use for a mere cripple. Especially one who is not morph-capable.>

"Blackmail?" I guessed.

<Yes. The visser used Mertil to find me and I offered to exchange myself for Mertil. After all, it was my fault that he was seen by a human. I should have protected him more carefully. But Mertil anticipated my action. In an effort to save my life he informed the visser of my medical condition.> Gafinilan laughed roughly. <The visser has no more use for an Andalite with a several-month life expectancy than he does for a *vecol*.>

<I suppose you could be grateful for that,> Cassie commented.

Gafinilan turned an eye stalk in her direction. <We all want to be wanted,> he remarked quietly.

"The visser still wants something from you," Jake said.

<Oh, yes. Visser Three is quite clever. And quite cruel. He has offered me a trade. If I bring him a healthy, morph-capable Andalite, he will release Mertil to me.>

<And you trust him?> Rachel spat.

<What choice do I have? Trust and act, or do nothing and wait for news of Mertil's murder. When I unexpectedly encountered young Aximili, I did not hesitate to bait my trap —>

Ax interrupted. <You are willing to betray one of your own people to the Yeerks in exchange for your friend's life? For the life of a mere *vecol*?>

<For me,> Gafinilan stated, <it is not about action traitorous to my world. For me, it is personal. It is about friendship.>

CHAPTER 17

"Let's do it. Let's rescue Mertil and kick some Yeerk butt."

Big guess who said that.

We all demorphed and Jake introduced us to Gafinilan. He explained Tobias and strongly suggested to Gafinilan — with a swift glance at all of us — that we join forces to recover Mertil.

<There is no need for you to further involve yourselves in this situation,> Gafinilan replied, almost harshly. <Mertil is my responsibility.>

I shook my head. I wasn't totally buying Gafinilan's story, not without proof, but I knew that his going in alone was ridiculous. And potentially dangerous for us. My vote? Don't let this guy out of our sight. "What are you going to do all by yourself?" I said. "Against Visser Three and masses of Hork-Bajir shock troops?"

"No offense, Gafinilan," Jake added. "But you're in no shape to act alone. The odds are against you even without your being sick."

"Besides," Cassie said gently, "you and Mertil are here on Earth because you were fighting to protect us. The human race. Consider it a favor if we help you rescue Mertil. Good karmic payback."

Tobias remained silent. Not unusual. He's unpredictably moody lately. But I was sure he was with the program.

Ax, too, declined to help convince Gafinilan to accept our assistance. I was pretty sure he was not with the program.

<But . . .> Gafinilan hesitated. <I cannot allow children to fight my battle. It would be unconscionable.>

Rachel rolled her eyes.

"No disrespect, Gafinilan," Jake said, "but we're going with you. Actually, you're going with us. So now, you play by our rules or you sit this one out."

If Gafinilan was stunned or offended by Jake's speech, he didn't show it. Exhaustion, depression — whatever it was — made him accept the situation with little or no resistance.

<Mertil is moved throughout the day and

night,> he said after a moment. <As far as I can tell, he is never in the same place for more than an hour, and has never been in the same place twice.>

"Why not just keep him in the Yeerk pool complex?" Rachel asked. "Plenty of empty cages, torture equipment, stuff like that."

<I imagine the visser is afraid of attack,> Gafinilan answered. <I imagine he does not trust me to complete our bargain. I imagine he half expects me to join up with the guerrilla forces that plague his efforts. Which, it seems, I have just done.>

"So, Mertil's in some sort of transport vehicle," Cassie said. "A truck, a horse trailer, something. How do we find it? Aerial surveillance . . ."

Ax interrupted, <We cannot risk our lives for a *vecol*.>

"Okay, Ax-man," I said, my voice a little less than steady. "I've been cutting you slack on this handicapped thing because you're part of the team. But when you talk like that, like this guy is some sort of dirty, worthless thing, I have to say you're just not one of us."

<I do not and have never pretended to be human,> Ax stated.

Rachel snorted. "You're so full of it, Marco. I seem to recall your calling that Hewlett Aldershot guy who was in a coma a vegetable. No, wait, a carrot, to be exact."

"Not the same thing," I shot back. "That was black comedy. Gallows humor. Not an open or implied insult."

"Actions do speak louder than words," Cassie said quietly.

"Thank you. I might not always say the right thing, but most times I do the right thing. Or try to, at least. My intentions," I added, smirking, "are good."

<This is not about Marco,> Tobias said. <This is about Mertil. Mertil is Gafinilan's *shorm,* Ax. Can't you understand . . .>

"Whether Ax understands or not," Jake interrupted, "we're doing this. Is *that* understood? Good. Gafinilan, you've been in contact with Mertil?"

During our verbal skirmish, Gafinilan had remained silent. Maybe he was tired of having to defend his position.

<Mertil and I have been the closest of friends since our childhood,> he said finally. <Unless we are on different planets, we can hear each other's thought-speak. Not perfectly. Often exact words are not clear. But the sound of Mertil's voice is always with me. It helps me to know he is alive.>

"So, what?" Rachel said. "Bird morphs, cover every inch of the town until we get close enough to Mertil for Gafinilan to hear specifics? Hope Mertil has been able, at least, to get a glimpse out a window or something."

CHAPTER 18

I understand ruthless.

I understand, maybe more than any of the others, what it means to be unsentimental. Cold, even. To see the end in the beginning and the beginning in the end.

I'm not denying that Jake, for example, doesn't make his share of tough decisions. That almost every day he isn't forced to choose between two seemingly impossible, equally degrading choices. That he doesn't feel the agony of those crisis moments. That too often he looks about fifty.

All I'm saying is that I understand, immediately and on some instinctual level, the state of ruthlessness you have to reach — almost, to live

in — to be able to make those impossible choices. To see the right way to the right end.

To accept being perceived as cruel and heartless.

To live with the fact that people are afraid of getting too close to someone like me, like maybe it'll rub off, my ability to do what needs to be done.

In spite of my incredible sense of humor, I am not always fun to be around. And there are a lot of reasons why. What would you be like if you had to decide whether to save what was left of your mother's life? Or let Visser One, the Yeerk, live? Calculated risk. I still don't know the results of that particularly agonizing decision, but I'd been able to do it. Been able to *make* the decision.

So, on some level, I knew what Gafinilan was all about. How he'd made the impossible decision to do whatever it took to save his friend's life. Even if that meant sacrificing his own. Even if that meant handing over another Andalite, one of his own people, to the Yeerks.

It was a pretty ruthless thing to do. And I was pretty sure he would do it again if he had to.

I respected him for that.

<Jake.> I spoke privately. <You'd better be aware we are in serious doo-doo if this guy decides to trade loyalties . . .>

<Marco. We're doing this.>

<Fine. I'm here. But let's be clear. What Gafinilan was saying is that he was ready to betray us. What's changed? Okay, he can't fulfill his part of the bargain with the visser. Can't deliver an adult Andalite. But maybe he can cut a new deal, if things start going bad. Hand over the human "Andalite bandits" in exchange for Mertil.>

<He said he'd work with us, not against us,> Jake said, tiredly.

<You believe that. I'll believe the opposite. That way we have all bases covered.>

<Fine. Let's get this over with.>

Gafinilan was in an owl morph he'd picked up a while back. I was an owl. Cassie was osprey. Jake, peregrine falcon. Rachel, bald eagle and Ax northern harrier. Tobias, of course, was himself.

For the past half hour we'd been flying north of town in a widespread group. Hoping to find a trace of Mertil. So far, radio silence.

<Mertil says he is in some sort of graveyard.> Gafinilan's thought-speak was sudden and excited.

<Impossible.> Rachel. <There are no graveyards out this way. That I know of, anyway.>

<Warehouses, yes . . .>

<He said that when his Hork-Bajir guards opened the door of his current prison, he was able to glimpse several large, boxlike, rectangu-

lar vehicles, somewhat similar to the one in which he is being held. They are made of metal, but rusted. Mertil assumes they have been abandoned.>

<Got it,> I said. <The old train yard. About a mile out from here.>

The old train yard and final station stop had not been in operation since, like, my grandmother was a kid. Now, it was only a vast arena of sharp edges from which to get lockjaw. A place where teenagers hung and had wild parties and did things they could get arrested for.

We reached the acre or so of dilapidated metal train parts. And saw nothing you wouldn't expect to see in such a place. Even with my superior owl vision, I could make out no suspicious footprints in the dirt or tufts of blue fur stuck to jagged pieces of boxcar.

And the place was quiet. Too quiet.

I circled lower, hoping for some shred of evidence that Mertil was being held on this site. Again, nothing. Hundreds of empty boxcars, each sixty feet long. The occasional caboose or flatcar. Some cattle cars lying on their sides. A locomotive or two.

<Nothing,> I said disgustedly. <Rust, rats, and empty cars.>

<Gafinilan, do you still hear Mertil?> Jake asked. <Are you sure he's here?>

<Yes, yes. He is close.>

<Okay then, people. We're going to have to land, morph some firepower, get our hands dirty.>

<Is it me,> I asked generally, <or does Jake sound like a deranged camp director when he talks like that?>

<It's you.> Cassie. The girlfriend. Figured.

Just then —

<About three o'clock everyone!> I called.

The door to one of the abused boxcars was sliding open. And the boxcar was disgorging about a dozen Hork-Bajir.

Another car! And another dozen Hork-Bajir.

Oh, yeah. There was definitely something there.

CHAPTER 19

Night was falling fast. Maybe the mass of clustered, hulking railroad cars added to the sense of gloom that seemed to be descending over the old yard and station.

The place had the eerie feel of all abandoned scenes of once-frenzied human activity. In a sense, Mertil was right when he called it a graveyard. No more hustling conductors and scurrying maintenance men. No more excited passengers and no more fretful family members, waiting for those passengers to disembark.

Now it really was the end of the line. Thick with shadows thrown by a few dim and distant roadway lights. And within those murky shadows, huge, shuffling Hork-Bajir.

We landed on the far east of the yard, atop a right-side-up passenger car. From there, we could watch the Yeerk shock troops undetected. Watch as they streamed through the mazelike paths between rusted-out corpses and gathered in a small clearing almost exactly at the yard's center.

Watch as they loosely surrounded a fifteen-foot U-Haul truck, the self-rental kind.

<I'm thinking Mertil's probably in that U-Haul. And that they're gonna be moving him pretty soon,> I said.

<Yes.> Gafinilan paused. <Mertil believes this to be true. He has overheard some of his captors discussing the next destination. But he has no details.>

<Tobias?> Jake said. <Stay up top. We're going to need you to guide us toward that clearing once we're on the ground. Everybody else? Battle morphs. I'm thinking we're going to have to bust Mertil out the hard way.>

<What about Gafinilan?> Ax asked stiffly. <With all due respect, you are not well . . .>

<I will fight. That is, if your prince will allow me to join you.>

<Great,> Jake said. <But if you feel you can't hold out, lay low. I don't want to have to rescue two Andalites tonight. Ax? Keep close to Gafinilan in case he needs help.> Jake paused. <Or in case he decides to switch sides.>

Gafinilan didn't respond to Jake's statement. Either he really was a good soldier, acknowledging Jake as his prince. Or he was even more calculating than I'd assumed.

We glided off the roof of the car and demorphed. Then I went gorilla, with cinder-block fists. Jake to tiger, with deadly claws and teeth. Cassie to wolf, lithe and tireless. Rachel used her elephant morph, perfect for bulldozing and busting through pesky walls of metal. Ax and Gafinilan stayed Andalite.

Suddenly . . .

<You must go.> It was a thought-speak voice I didn't recognize. Soft and sad. A broken voice. The voice of someone after the boredom and shame of capture sets in.

Mertil.

Truth is, sure, leaving would have been no problem. I'm not stupid enough to get all excited about wading into bloody battle, four kids, a bird, two aliens — one mortally ill and possibly traitorous — against a good hundred Hork-Bajir soldiers.

I glanced at Gafinilan. He was holding tightly to the rusted axle of a caboose. Breathing shallowly.

<Gafinilan?> I said. <Tell Mertil we'll see him in a few.>

<Tobias,> Jake said. <We're ready. Which way to the clearing?>

Way up in the dark sky, Tobias, our own perfect wilderness guide, said, <There's a red caboose dead ahead. Circle it to the left. If I say it's clear, continue on past the next car.>

We lumbered and stalked and trotted forward. Through the maze of looming abandoned hulks. Tobias guided us until we were within a few dozen yards of the clearing. And, by the light of a smallish bonfire the Hork-Bajir had just built, we could see all too clearly just how outnumbered we were.

<Gee, Jake, have the odds ever been this bad?> I asked brightly.

<Sure,> Jake answered. <But this time we've got the element of surprise.>

"Andalite!"

<Oh, crap.>

Not even Tobias is perfect. Up on top of a railway car stood a Hork-Bajir. Pointing a bladed arm down at us.

<He must have scrambled up the other side!> Tobias called. <It's too dark!>

Sirens. Frenzied commands. The ominous sound of Hork-Bajir blades against metal.

So much for the element of surprise.

CHAPTER 20

"Aaahhh!"

The Hork-Bajir hurled himself from the top of the car.

<Rachel! It's your soulmate!>

One lone Hork-Bajir, tearing at the seven of us, blades flashing.

WHUMPF!

He hit the ground when Gafinilan smacked him with the side of his enormous tail blade.

<He is unconscious,> the Andalite said. <I believe he will remain so for some time.>

<Duh.>

<Everyone!> Jake. <We're not going to stand

here and wait for the rest of them to show up. Stick to the shadows. We move forward and surround the clearing.>

<Too late, man,> Tobias reported. <They're sending out a unit of Hork-Bajir. They'll be on you in a minute!>

<Okay, new plan. Wait until they're close,> Jake snapped. <Then we take them down.>

<What about the next batch, after them?> Cassie cried.

<Take them down, too. We've got to keep pushing closer to the clearing.>

<And Mertil,> Gafinilan said quietly.

<Look out!>

Out of the gloom, ten Hork-Bajir, charging ahead. Too late to hide.

One came right at me. I ducked and slammed both fists into its belly.

WWHUMP!

He fell down.

"Rrroooooooaaar!"

Jake! With outstanding speed and agility he leaped forward. The force of the seven-hundred-pound Siberian tiger slammed two more Yeerk warriors onto the ground.

FWAAP! FWAAP!

Ax. Fighting alongside Gafinilan, he was even more amazing than usual.

A wolf's howl!

<Cassie, you okay?>

<Yeah.> Trotting away from a fallen Hork-Bajir. <He nicked me but I got him.>

"Tseeeer!"

Yes! Tobias. A howling Hork-Bajir clutched the red mess that had once been his eyes.

Rachel. Wrapping her trunk around a Hork-Bajir and . . .

THUWUUUMP!

Tossing him somewhere into the gloom.

This was too easy. Something . . .

More! Another five, ten warriors descending on us.

<Spread out!> Jake ordered. <Make them think we've got them surrounded.>

<Now that's optimistic,> I said.

I dodged left. Slipped into the shadows.

A moment later, leaped out onto the back of a Hork-Bajir. Wrestled him to the ground.

<Aaahh!>

Before I could get to my feet, my victim's buddy brought his elbow blade down onto my shoulder.

It went deep.

FWAAP!

Gafinilan!

<Thanks, man,> I said, wrenching the de-

tached blade of the now incapacitated Hork-Bajir from tendon and muscle.

<You are welcome, Marco,> he replied. <But I would advise you to watch your back more closely.>

I swear if the guy had a mouth he would have been grinning.

<I will,> I promised.

The cut was bad but I'd lived through worse.

<Marco!> Rachel cried. <A little help, please! I can't turn around in here!>

I knuckle-ran over to Rachel. Somehow she'd gotten herself in a too-narrow alley between train cars.

I tore the Hork-Bajir from her flank. Flung him behind me, into the side of a caboose.

<Back out, Rachel. I'll watch your, uh . . .>

<Don't say it,> she snapped. <Just don't say it.>

But I was already gone, hurling oncoming Hork-Bajir left and right. The wound on my shoulder throbbing, my head now bleeding, too. I touched the damage and felt bone.

It was so dark and suddenly, there were so, so many.

I stumbled, backed away from the Hork-Bajir coming ever closer. Trapping me in a small corner from which there'd be no way out.

I realized I'd lost Jake and the others, though I could hear their grunts and howls through the terrible roar and brittle clash of battle.

Okay, I thought crazily, *I got myself into this. Now I'll get myself out.*

The question was how.

CHAPTER 21

<I am Kong!>

I bellowed! Pounded my fists against my gorilla chest. It was a display of totally false machismo.

But it worked.

Gave me the split second I needed to slip through the partially open door of a boxcar, slam it shut behind me.

Scramble across the dirty floor, bumpy with rat droppings and crunchy with broken glass, and tear open the door on the other side of the car.

Drop to the ground, slam the door shut behind me.

Take a deep breath . . .

Uh-oh.

And realize I was facing another onslaught of Hork-Bajir.

Hard to tell exactly how far away in the heavy dark.

I leaned up against the side of the car. Held perfectly still.

Hoped the gorilla's dark hair and skin would help camouflage me. Keep me hidden, just a darker spot in the shadows.

When you're a kid, you know how you close your eyes and convince yourself that because you're blind you're also invisible?

Well, it doesn't work when you're surrounded by seven-foot-tall, horned and bladed lizardlike enemies.

Hork-Bajir vision isn't spectacular in the dark, but their hearing is keen. From the beating of my heart and the hot breaths pumping in and out of my nostrils, they'd know I was here.

I got ready to start swinging.

And then . . .

Something made me glance to my right, almost over my torn shoulder.

A ladder rung. Built into the train car wall.

Maybe I could grasp it, swing out from it, adding force to my punches and kicks.

Unless . . .

A ladder rung is part of a ladder.

Ladders lead to places where you are not.

The first two Hork-Bajir were on me! I grabbed them by the necks and smashed them together. The daggerlike horns on their heads stabbed into each other's flesh. Got stuck.

Then, as the next two Hork-Bajir skidded to a stop a few feet from their fallen buddies, I scrambled up the ladder.

Ignored the searing pain in my shoulder.

And was almost immediately on top of the train car.

Fantastic! From here I could see the clearing. The remains of the bonfire and the U-Haul truck, still parked.

But not for long.

<Everyone!> I screamed. <They're moving the truck!>

And we were still too far from the clearing to stop it.

Maybe . . . if we headed toward the main entrance, maybe we could cut it off before it hit open road.

Maybe.

<I'm going for the main gate!> I called. <Whoever can, meet me there!>

<Where the heck is the main gate?> It was Rachel.

Good question. I scanned the old train yard.

Spotted the dark hulk of the old station. Figured that the parking lot for cars would have been close to the station. Convenience. Figured the main entrance/exit would lead off the parking lot.

<Okay,> I shouted, <all the way left. Probably behind the old station. Just go!>

<I'll follow the headlights,> Tobias said.

<Ax is back with Gafinilan,> Jake cried. <He's losing it. We're down two soldiers so look sharp.>

Going overland was definitely the way.

Thud thud thud thud . . .

I made my way to the other end of the roof. The roof of the next train car to the left was about ten feet away. Too far for me to jump.

I scanned. Okay. There was another way across the tops of the cars. A way that would get me close to if not right at the old station house. A slightly circuitous path, a weird, twisting metal road over a sea of battle. If I weren't stopped by Hork-Bajir, I could make it before the U-Haul left the yard.

If . . .

Thud thud thud thud . . .

Closer. Roof to roof. Moving ahead, then, slowly, bit by bit, to the left, toward the station.

<Marco!> Tobias called. <You're gonna intercept the truck in about a minute. Hurry!>

Thudthudthudthud . . .

<Marco, I'm just behind you, on the ground,> Rachel said.

<You're on your own, Marco!> Jake. <Cassie and I got caught up by a few Hork-Bajir. We're . . .>

Jake's thought-speak disappeared.

A light. Two. Round and small. Yeah, there was the truck, moving slowly with only its own headlights to guide it. I dropped close against the roof of the train car. Crawled the last few feet to the edge.

And prepared to drop onto the roof of the truck.

<When I give the word, buddy,> Tobias called.

<I'm on it.>

<Go! Go! Go!>

I flew! Launched my big gorilla body down onto the metal roof of the U-Haul.

WHUMMPF!

Landed in a crouch and allowed my weight to fall quickly to the side.

Safe.

And still only going about twenty miles an hour.

<Driver heard something,> Tobias reported.

Well, duh. I'd left a big ole dent in the metal roofing. This was a surprise attack.

I crawled forward across the cargo bay and

onto the roof of the truck's cabin. Peered over the side into the driver's seat. Saw a very nervous human-Controller.

I tore open his door. Reached for him.

Too slow! The driver slammed on the brakes.

The truck stopped moving.

I didn't.

CHAPTER 22

Forty feet through the air!

WHOOF!

I hit the ground. Rolled another twenty.

Finally, came to a stop. And not a pretty one, let me tell you.

Hurt but alive.

Thanked the stars for the helmetlike gorilla skull.

SCREEEEEEEE!

The driver hit the gas!

Now he was going to hit the gorilla.

Closer! Closer!

The grill of the truck loomed.

The stench of burning rubber.

I scrambled unsteadily to my feet.

Then . . .

CRAAAAAASSSHHH!

A train car! It smashed right into the path of the speeding truck, stopping it dead.

Above the sizzling wreckage I heard Rachel's trumpet of triumph.

<Nice, Rachel.> I knuckle-walked toward the smash. <Get Mertil into a train wreck.>

<You're welcome for saving your life,> she replied. <Again.>

The cab of the truck was completely impacted. A twisted and bent remnant. The front two wheels were off the ground, resting on the top of the flattened boxcar.

The driver's door was open. I don't know how he managed to survive the crash. But he had and he'd been Yeerk enough to get away.

<Mertil!> I called, loping around to the back of the truck, now in real blackness again because the truck's headlights were destroyed. <You okay?>

<I am as I was.>

Great. Another Mr. Philosophy.

<Let's get this open,> Rachel said. <Before the gas tank blows or something.>

I wrapped my thick gorilla fingers around the gate latch on the back of the truck and pulled. Yanked.

Nothing. The muscles in my chest and arm strained as I tried again.

Still nothing. Now my shoulder was really on fire.

<Let me try my trunk,> Rachel said.

<Be my guest,> I muttered.

<Marco! Rachel!>

It was Jake, slinking out of the shadows, bloody, but I'd seen him worse. Cassie, Ax, and Gafinilan were with him. Each bearing evidence of the fight.

A second later, Tobias fluttered silently to the top of a nearby caboose.

<We're trying to get Mertil out,> Rachel explained.

Gafinilan stepped forward. <Is he . . . ?>

<I am fine, Gafinilan,> Mertil answered. <Though still in this box.>

<I will open the truck,> Gafinilan said.

He moved into place directly behind and facing the rear door.

CLAAAANG!

I jumped. Couldn't help it, the sound was enormous.

Gafinilan's battle-ax tail blade had punctured the steel door.

The guy might be dying, but he was still inconceivably strong.

SKKREEEEEEUUUUULLLL!

Cassie's wolf whimpered involuntarily at the awful sound of Gafinilan's tail blade tearing a long gash down the steel door.

<Very cool,> Rachel said.

When he'd created a sort of tall, elliptical slit, Gafinilan stepped back.

WHAM! WHAM! WHAM!

And Mertil kicked his way out.

CHAPTER 23

We had found Mertil. Probably saved his life.

His dear friend Gafinilan had gone to terrible lengths to set him free.

Mertil must have been pleased. On some level, in some way. But he didn't look all that happy.

We were in the woods. Far safer than hanging around the train yard, waiting for a stray Hork-Bajir-Controller to find us.

<I am surprised,> Mertil said plainly, <that you were willing to risk your lives for me. As I am.>

He held the stump of his tail down, as flat as it could go against his body. As if he were ashamed. The position had to be uncomfortable.

<We don't know what you mean,> Cassie said kindly.

<I will explain,> Ax said. <He means he is surprised that we normal, healthy warriors risked our lives for a mere *vecol.*> He paused. Turned a stalk eye to me and added, <Or, as Marco says, someone who is "differently abled.">

<Jeez, can't we just get over this issue, please?> Rachel said. <It's not like it's Mertil's fault he got injured. Or that he has an allergy or something. Man, I can name a few people I know who are perfectly healthy and a total waste of oxygen. In my opinion.>

<I'm down with that,> I murmured.

Mertil and Gafinilan remained silent.

<Ax,> Jake said. <You consider Gafinilan a hero of Andalite culture. Right?>

Ax nodded. One of his favorite adopted human gestures.

<Maybe the fact that he's able to overlook physical imperfection is one of the reasons he's a hero. What do you think?>

<Prince Jake, I think the reason Gafinilan is able to overlook his friend's deformities is because he sees through the eyes of friendship. This is exceptional behavior. Under ordinary circumstances, in general Andalite society, it is simply not natural to show such concern for a *vecol.*>

<So, friendship isn't natural?> Rachel snapped. <It's abnormal?>

<What is "normal," anyway?> Cassie asked, rhetorically.

<The norm. The standard. The average,> I said.

Tobias glared. <Okay, I'm getting a complex over here. I'm a *nothlit*. A freak. Whatever. My best friend is an alien with blue fur. My girlfriend is human — when she isn't in morph. How about we don't talk about "normal" anymore. Or "average" or "natural." Please.>

More weird silence. I, for one, was dying to hear what would happen next.

<Mertil-Iscar-Elmand,> Ax said. Respectfully. <It has been an honor to meet you. I will always remember you as you were.>

Well, it was a start.

<We should get out of here,> Jake said. <Gafinilan, we'll help you and Mertil get back.>

<Thank you.>

And again I saw the trembling I'd seen before. Only worse. And I remembered Gafinilan's not being sure he'd seen the human me that first night. Peering closely at his own printed labels in the greenhouse. He was going blind.

When the trembling ceased, Gafinilan went on. <And then, you will be so kind as to let us be. My time is running out. I would like to end my

days honorably and in the company of my dearest friend.>

Mertil, who was no lousy specimen of Andalite warrior himself, stood tall. <As Gafinilan has cared for me, so now I will care for him. It is my duty.>

<The visser might not leave you alone,> Jake pointed out.

<The visser has proven he has no use for either of us,> Gafinilan retorted.

<He's right, Jake,> I said. <If the visser comes after anyone it'll be us. For spoiling his plans.>

<Oh, goody,> Cassie said dryly. <You always know how to finish on a high note, Marco.>

<Thank you,> I said.

CHAPTER 24

You know that old party game, "Who Am I This Time?" Or that nursery rhyme about a doctor, lawyer, baker. Whatever. People tend to get identified by what kind of hat they wear during the day. By what is visible, noticeable, obvious about them.

So, if you've got one arm or get around in a wheelchair or are blind, you're a handicapped person. Maybe you're also a poet or scholar, a sinner, or a saint. But first and foremost in people's minds, you're handicapped.

Not a lot you can do about it, either.

My mother is — was? — host to Visser One. Originator of the Yeerk invasion of Earth.

Everyone, including my dad and his new wife, thinks she's dead.

Maybe she is.

Maybe she isn't.

Maybe she can be saved.

Maybe she can't.

I just don't know, after the last time we came face-to-face. In a Taxxon tunnel off the main Yeerk pool. During her trial by the Council of Thirteen.

Most times, I don't even pretend to want to know. Though if a call comes again . . .

Well, I'll wait until that happens to decide. And then I'll do what I have to do.

Anyway, for the time being, I am "the boy with a dead mother" to people on the outside. To my friends, I'm "the kid with the big mouth and mother stolen by aliens."

Can't get away from it.

Vecol, mentally challenged, handicapped. Dumb, psycho, gimp.

You just learn to live with it.

Jake's the responsible leader.

Rachel's the gorgeous warmonger.

Cassie's the tree-hugger.

Tobias, Bird-boy.

Ax, resident alien.

Gafinilan is the one with the fatal disease.

Mertil . . .

So we rescued Mertil and agreed to leave him

and Gafinilan in peace. We were pretty sure the Yeerks were going to back away from them, too. At least for a while.

I mean, like Gafinilan said, what had either Andalite done for them? Nothing. Except exhibit a depth of loyalty totally puzzling, totally incomprehensible to Visser Three and his minions.

So given the fact that in the Yeerk opinion Gafinilan was, essentially, a dead man and Mertil useless, we figured they stood a fair chance of living unmolested.

At least until Gafinilan died and Mertil was all alone in Henry McClellan's house. Unable to morph. A virtual prisoner in a foreign land.

How would he survive?

Maybe I shouldn't have done it . . .

How often do I say that? A lot.

Maybe I shouldn't have done it, but I did.

Paid one last, unauthorized visit to the McClellan house. In osprey morph, and while Gafinilan/Henry was at work.

I am not totally stupid.

I found Mertil in the greenhouse. Called out to him from a distance so he wouldn't be scared and zap me with a shredder or something. Identified myself as the handsome gorilla from the other night.

<The others don't know I'm here, so, uh, I'd appreciate it if this visit is our little secret.>

<Of course,> Mertil answered, his voice a bit strained. <I believe I owe you my life.>

<Well, I don't know about that,> I said. <But, look. I just want you to know — I mean, we just want you to know that if . . . uh, when Gafinilan, you know, dies. That you should look us up. And, well, maybe I can check in on you, too. Play some video games, whatever. Being alone, man, it's not good and . . . well, we could use all the allies we can get.>

Nothing. I shifted on my perch in the big old oak tree where Tobias had sat during our first visit to the house.

Noted a honeybee winging its way toward the greenhouse.

Waited.

Maybe I'd offended the guy somehow. I hadn't meant to but sometimes my mouth gets in the way of sentiment.

The silence was awful.

And then, suddenly, his voice came booming out at me. Strong and energetic and quivering with something that sounded a lot like pride.

<Thank you, *Aristh* Marco. Perhaps I will do so.>

Don't miss

#41 The Familiar

DEE-DEET! DE-DEET!

The alarm was like a jackhammer to the head. I groaned.

DE-DEET!

Enough, already! I felt for the clock radio. The snooze button. Just five more minutes.

My hand patted the air vainly. No bedside table? I lifted my lids. Where was my . . .

My heart stopped.

I was staring into a triangular screen. A flat computer panel mounted flush in a peeling, white plaster wall across from the bed. Eerie copper letters pulsed at the top of the glowing gray screen. 5:28:16 A.M. Below the time flashed the words "TO DO" and a single entry: "Report to work."

This was not my room. Not even close.

DE-DEET! DE-DEET!

My body stiffened to warrior mode and I bolted out of bed.

The alarm broke off.

My mind, forced back into consciousness by the shock, hurled me orders. "Get out!" it warned. "Get out, get out, get out!"

I raced to a tall black panel in the wall. A door. Had to be.

Get out!

I tried, but there was no handle. No release lever. Nothing.

I struck it.

"You are not prepared to leave for work!" said a shrill computer voice.

I pounded even harder. Hammered the panel with a clenched fist. A fist that . . .

I stopped suddenly as I studied my fist.

It was big.

I mean it was rough and callused and had veins that pumped across the hairy, muscular forearm like I belonged to Powerhouse Gym and actually used my membership.

It was the arm of a grown man.

My heart started up again, pumping now at record speed.

I probed the polished steel door frame for my reflection, for the face I knew.

And yes, there! I saw my eyes, dark as midnight. My strong, broad face. My . . .

I swallowed hard.

My short-cropped hair? My six-foot frame?

My day-old beard?

I brought a hand to my face. My fingers scraped across my chin. Stubble like sixty-grit sandpaper. I needed a shave.

My breath got choppy. My head felt about ready to explode.

The Jake staring back at me was an adult! Not crazy old. But out of college a few years. At least ten years older than the kid I'd been the night before.

What was going on? Where were the others? How did I get to this place?

I was gonna have a heart attack if I didn't calm down. I stumbled back to bed and sat down on the narrow strip no wider than a torso. A pad on a metal plate.

"Okay," I said out loud. "Okay." Use your brain. Cover the possible explanations.

An Ellimist trick? Yeah, it had to be. But why hadn't he spoken?

A Yeerk experiment, maybe? Could I have been captured?

It's hard to think straight when you wake up like Tom Hanks in that movie *Big*. At least he woke up in his own room, in his own clothes. Sort of. I was wearing this weird, faded orange jumpsuit, the color of a sun-bleached Orioles cap.

I fingered the suit, and then it hit me.

Of course!

I knew what was going on here. It had finally happened.

I knew it was only a matter of time, what with the pressures of leadership, the violent battle, the endless fights against a strengthening enemy.

I'd finally been driven to a complete psychotic breakdown.

And this was my padded cell.

<THE FUTURE IS HERE...AND IT'S TERRIFYING>

ANIMORPHS®

K. A. Applegate

It was a night like any other when Jake went to bed as his usual kid-self. He wakes up the next morning to find himself ten years older, a full-grown adult in a world completely overtaken by Yeerks! Are the other Animorphs still alive—or will Jake have to find a way to fight alone?

ANIMORPHS #41: THE FAMILIAR

Visit the Web site at: www.scholastic.com/animorphs

ANIT999

<Imagine a World Without Animorphs>

ANIMORPHS®

<MEGAMORPHS #4>

Every leader has a breaking point, even Jake.

After a grisly battle, a Drode offers him an escape from the terrifying pressure. Jake accepts.

Now, there's no morphing, no missions, and no knowledge of the Yeerks. But Jake and the others discover that you can't close your eyes to the truth you know is out there.

MEGAMORPHS #4: BACK TO BEFORE

Coming in APRIL!

MEG999

Visit the Web site at: http://www.scholastic.com/animorphs